LIONEL LANCET
AND THE RIGHT VIBE

Daniel Backer

Acknowledgments

Thank you to Miruna Voican, Vincent Degaetano, Matthew Justus Falkum, Robert McCormack, Tory Baxter, and Joe Backer. You all read the manuscript multiple times over the past four years and played a critical role in its development. Special thanks to Madeline Krane, Kari C., Aaron Fronk, Marilyn Hammond, Kyle Johnson, Sierra Reed, Ross Kenyon, and Rick Homuth for your insightful feedback. Each of you provided invaluable notes that made the story come to life. Thank you to Phillip Freedenberg, Rick Harsch, and Noah Clemons for promoting my work and connecting me to an amazing internet community. Thank you to Conor Reed for your excellent work on the cover art. And lastly, thank you to Diana Backer for your support and encouragement.

Dear Reader,

This is an independently published work of fiction that relies on word of mouth promotion and recommendations from readers like you. Please consider sharing a photo of *Lionel Lancet and the Right Vibe* or a video of you reading a few lines from the book. Tagging the author in a social media post or writing a simple review is immensely helpful.

—Daniel Backer

Tiktok & Instagram: @danielbackerauthor
YouTube: Off the Wall Novels
Goodreads: Daniel Backer
www.danielbacker.com

LIONEL LANCET
AND THE RIGHT VIBE

"The Self is everywhere."
—*Isha Upanishad*

Part I
Show Me a Sign

Chapter 1

Art Lancet died climbing out of a window in his cliffside home in Palos Verdes, California. He lay on his side with his pants down, facing the ocean, jaw open, wind freeing white hairs from his combover and blowing them into a clump like a cockatiel's plume. The tribal print kurta he wore had a scuff of dirt across the back, which would have mortified him if he were not already dead. He got it half price at a meditation retreat in Maui.

The legacy Art left amounted to the organization he created: the Fiduciary Royalties Association for United Donors. To anyone at the IRS, it was a charitable foundation with many ventures under its umbrella, one of which funded the development of pharmaceutical drugs in collaboration with the National Institutes of Health. But the foundation also functioned as an entity Art could defer to when anyone questioned his reputation. Rumors circulated that he had a veritable medicine cabinet full of other ventures that were off the books.

Art's passing marked the end of an era for the Fiduciary Royalties Association for United Donors. He steered the foundation since the Reagan years through every tax loophole and market fluctuation, and the United Donors, always rearing for their Fiduciary Royalties, were handsomely rewarded for their investments. Constant thriving imbued the group with a mystical air, invoked through contracts and rituals behind closed doors. But with its high priest dead, the numinous had been snuffed out, and the whole foundation declined into stiff corporate scrambling.

But the role that earned Art his money was far from the real him: a distant reverberation of the baby boom that allowed him to get caught up in the counterculture of the '60s before relenting to a more corporate vibe.

He meditated Om before all stock trades and occasionally dropped LSD. Almost anyone who met him heard about his encounter with the divine on four tabs before Francis was born, and during his midlife crisis, he started a manuscript for a self-help book called *Fee Here Now,* an attempt to combine Eastern spiritual wisdom with the guidelines of financial consulting, but he abandoned it after his wife left.

Art regularly added evidence to the case that he was a crier, mostly catalyzed by music. "My Sweet Lord" by George Harrison would come on, and he would put a hand on the shoulder of whoever stood closest to him as though he needed help standing, his head bowed down. Tears would well up in his eyes but never quite spill out. After the last jubilant "Hare Krishna" faded out, Art would compose himself, shaking his head, and return to earth as though he had no say in getting carried away, only to find himself disappointed that his hostage lost interest.

The machinations of increasing profits and dodging taxes seemed like a dry and lifeless pursuit, but Art felt it like music. The profits, unencumbered by regulations and taxes, soared like a hopeful melody. The effect of music is not its meaning, and profit is hardly about the number. It's the growth, the smooth upward curve, the sublime anticipation of climax as everything builds to a crescendo. The strictures of rationality and materialism faded away as his dividends racked up indefinitely like an infinite surplus sent from beyond the earthly plane, squeezing through the slivers of space between individual dollars.

The evening of his death, Art slept in his home office, drooling on the papers spread across his desk. Plaques with shiny nameplates and plastic corporate logos faced the entrance for visitors to see. A knock on his front door startled him awake, and a tax form stuck to his sunburned cheek when he raised his head. It drooped down and landed on the floor with the smallest of sounds.

The trellis outside the floor-to-ceiling windows diced the light from the sunset into a spotted pattern on the floor. Some of the spots disappeared, effaced by the silhouette of someone trying to peek inside. A moment later, there was another firm knock on the door. Art held his breath and shivered with an adrenaline tickle he hadn't felt since playing hide and seek as a boy.

The maid's footsteps sounded outside of the office. Art stage whispered, "Constance, don't answer it!"

Constance's irises blended in with her pupils and her mouth opened slightly, giving her an earnest, engaged expression. Hunched in his chair, Art heard her pass through the foyer and open the front door, and he risked a breath, smelling the musk of his cigar that had gone out in a white marble ashtray.

"I need to speak with Art Lancet," said the voice at the door. "Is he home?"

"Yes, please come in."

Art threw his hands up. After a moment of panic, he rolled his plump body out of his chair, and upon impact with the floor, vertigo gripped him and sent the parquetry pattern below squirming in his vision. He shuddered and gasped, struggling to get up.

Constance's knuckles rapped gently on the office door, followed by heavy pounding from the visitor, and Art began his pained crawl toward the only escape, a window on the southern wall. He bumped into the faded yellow surfboard propped against the window frame and barely managed to stop it from crashing down on top of him. It had been too long since he last took it down to Lunada Bay.

"Is everything okay?" called Constance through the door.

Trembling, Art climbed his hands up the wall and clasped the windowsill. With a moan, he rose to his feet and pressed the heels of his palms beneath the window's horizontal muntin, but it didn't budge. The latch was almost completely open but not enough. He bared his teeth at it for inhibiting his escape.

By the time the visitor pushed past Constance and entered the office, the window was open, Art's top half hung outside, and his large, bare rump was on display in a proud greeting. With a flop, his bottom half went over the ledge, and out he tumbled, landing on his back.

The house was a ranch, so he didn't fall very far, but the sudden exertion on his aged body sent spasms down his left arm. As the swelling energy in his chest intensified, he attempted to cry out, but the muscles in his torso contracted as if they were trying to prevent something from escaping his body. The small sound that managed to get out was a choked *cuh* from the back of his throat.

The visitor was none other than Melanie Bobbers, internet famous lawyer/vlogger, i.e. vlawger, wearing a sport coat, pinstripe slacks, and a fed up expression on her face. The icon for her vlawg *Little Miss ProseCute* depicted a minimal rendering of her in profile, the left side of her head shaved and her lips pursed in defiance. She enjoyed a substantial following that venerated her for confronting rich and powerful men, capturing her exploits with a hidden camera pinned in her lapel.

A small-time television director gave her an acting tip to strike more fear in her targets—just don't blink. She could go for several minutes now, dry-eyed and unrelenting. Her posture betrayed that she bent over books for years, so when she caught herself craning too far forward, she would shift her shoulders down and her head back, which she tried to do as nonchalantly as possible.

Melanie fought traffic from Highland Park to personally deliver a subpoena, rehearsing for an hour and a half what she would say as she served the papers. It was all for naught as Art presently lay convulsing on the ground.

In spite of occasional performative stargazing, Art enjoyed most of his waking life upright, allowing the comforting solidity of the earth to fill everything below the horizon and the enticing ethereal sky to hover above it as a neat symmetrical opposite in his field of view. But now it dawned on him, as he lay on his back, how much more territory the sky occupied, looking down on him as if he were a ladybug in its palm. The clouds and all that lay beyond them began to swirl into a withdrawn point, and he erupted in blubbering terror at being invited to enter. It had been waiting for him his entire life. A presence was with him now like a calm parent comforting a child who was afraid of something that carried no real threat.

Melanie scuffed her heel on the floor, and Constance panicked behind her, peering over her shoulder. Leaning out the window for a better view, Melanie adjusted the camera in her lapel. The sprinkler system turned on and speckled Art's khaki pants that were bunched around his ankles.

"We're in a drought, asshole."

She retreated to Art's rolling chair and chewed her cheek, indifferent to Constance climbing out of the window. Something in the corner of the room reflected a glint of light where the wainscoting met the wall unevenly behind a small table that held a black stone lingam. As Constance delivered chest compressions, her head bobbing in and out of view through the window, Melanie approached the corner and moved the table out of the way. There was a barely perceptible hinge that swung open, revealing a hidden compartment, and inside was a dagger with a serpent for a handle that was swallowing the bottom of the blade. Melanie positioned the camera to get a cinematic shot with a pleasing lens flare.

Art's heartbeat was synchronizing with the waves of the Pacific Ocean, and his hand loosened its grip on the land beneath him. The usual metaphysical gravity that rooted him comfortably in his body let go of him, and he began to slowly evaporate. But in his last lucid moment, he had the wherewithal to command his body one last time, turning his head away from the sky and pointing a trembling, accusatory finger at Constance. She stopped the chest compressions and shrank away from the scorn in his eyes. When he went limp, she wailed. The outline of Catalina Island was the last thing he saw, barely visible in the dark as the sun finally finished setting.

The remaining members of the Fiduciary Royalties Association for United Donors were the only attendees at Art's funeral. They congregated on short notice for a small ceremony with mournful hymns and Sanskrit prayers. A censer dangled from the hand of one of the men, effusing incense around the burial plot and headstone that read "Art Lancet 1937 - 2016." There was no priest presiding, and no one spoke of the subpoena, but it hung over their bowed heads like a spirit. As Art was lowered into the ground, a leaf blower started a few plots down.

A tall man in a navy suit straightened his tie and walked to his black Maserati at a quickened pace. He drove north on Highway 1, and fog rolled up from the ocean, obscuring the divide between the land and the sea, so the tide seemed to reach past its edge, threatening to wash everything away.

Chapter 2

Posting the footage of Art's heart attack would have been in poor taste, but Melanie did watch it twice before deleting it. She fetched another subpoena the next day, intent on serving the next Lancet in line, Art's son Francis, the president of his father's foundation, not to mention the recipient of huge payouts from its pharmaceutical deals. Inching down the 405 for the second day in a row, Melanie rehearsed what she would say while serving Francis the papers. Her fans preferred pithy one-liners to scathing indictments, so she settled on, "Looks like crime runs in the family." She smirked to herself. If all went well, she'd have a post-worthy video by evening.

Francis lived in a beautiful ranch-style house almost identical to his father's, with floor-to-ceiling windows on the western wall and the sunset filtering through the trellises. The only difference was the helicopter on the roof. This was not legal per se, but Francis convinced the Palos Verdes Police Department that it was an eccentric ornament rather than a means of transportation he had any intention of using.

Melanie rang the doorbell, and Francis, a blonde, chubby man in his late forties, wearing a bathrobe, peered out of the window next to the front door. Recognizing her, he dashed away from the window. She rang the doorbell over and over until another Lancet, Francis's son Lionel, plump and short, in an identical bathrobe, came to the door and opened it for her.

"Is that recording?" said Lionel, pointing to the camera in her lapel.

"I need to speak to Francis Lancet," said Melanie. Lionel blocked the view of her camera with his hand. "Why are you trying to grab my breast?"

"Ah," said Lionel, withdrawing his hand as if he touched a hot surface.

"Get Francis right now."

"Dad," said Lionel. "There's an angry woman at the door."

They waited for Francis in silence, but he did not come.

"He's not home," said Lionel.

"Yes, he is," said Melanie, raising her voice. "I just saw him."

"Can we bring the energy down a little bit?" said Lionel. "Why didn't you talk to him when you saw him?"

"Because he's a coward. Can I speak with your mom?"

"She ran away with a bullfighter."

Salvatore, the man that Lionel's mom Amelia left with, was indeed from Spain, but being a bullfighter was only a joke that Francis and Lionel took at face value. Salvatore actually said, "In Spain, we are all bullfighters." Francis and Lionel didn't know any better. Also, to say that Amelia ran away undercut the boldness with which Salvatore informed Francis that they were leaving "to more fully realize the potential of [their] passionate sexual relationship."

"Go get your dad."

Lionel said, "Dad," into the house in a whine that turned the word into two syllables. Turning back to Melanie, he shrugged. "I guess he left."

"He didn't leave. He's avoiding responsibility."

Melanie pushed past him and entered the house, and Lionel recoiled, violated less by her intrusion than by her touching him.

"Francis Lancet, I know you're home."

The open floor plan allowed her to see into the living room, kitchen, and sitting rooms from the foyer. Clothes lay scattered about, and judging by the smell, fruit rotted somewhere. A flat-screen TV that had never been hung leaned against the wall facing a couch with a deep indent in one of the cushions, and wadded napkins, half-drunk soda bottles, and take-out boxes balanced on the armrests. Framed in the center of the living room wall was a naked woman drenching herself with a hose. Melanie scoffed.

With the Californian upward inflection as a substitute for polite dismissal, Lionel said, "I'm kind of in the middle of something."

"What? Jacking off?"

Lionel blushed, framed perfectly in Melanie's hidden camera. She could edit the wadded napkins and poster of the naked woman next to this footage and let her fans draw their own conclusions.

Flustered, Lionel took a moment to apprehend this total stranger who just barged into his house. He saw her pain and exhaustion from having to uphold her stern determination. An odd desire arose to comfort her, but he tensed his body, forcing the sensation down until it disappeared.

A whooshing sound started from overhead, and they both froze to listen. It was coming from outside. Melanie sprinted out the open front door to get a better look, and Lionel joined her on the lawn. The propellers of the helicopter on the roof were gathering speed, the downdraft flattening the grass and whipping the flowers about. Francis sat in the pilot's seat, flipping switches and adjusting dials.

"I'm sorry, Lionel," said Francis through a megaphone. "This is goodbye. I'm not coming back. I left a fifty in my office for some pizzas. Be good." With that, he rose into the sky over Lionel who squinted up at him and Melanie who stared in disbelief. Before long, his house became small, and the wide cove beneath him looked like just another bite mark in the cliffs.

The pulsing propeller noises dissipated, and there was a moment of calm. Lionel looked to Melanie for what to do next. Although he was twenty-six, he regarded her as the adult present. Neighbors came out on their porches and looked out over the ocean, using their hands as visors.

Melanie's face hardened, and she futzed with the camera in her lapel. Lionel was never great with exits, having been known to quietly slink away on rare occasions he found himself at small gatherings, and he started toward the door as casually as possible.

"You're a Lancet," said Melanie, shifting her head in a sudden movement and locking her glare on Lionel.

"Yes?" said Lionel, turning to face her.

"This was meant for your grandfather and then for your father, but now all I have is you. So here goes." Melanie went off script, saying, "You are a vile, wicked human. You have no love in your heart, and everything you have ever done is a lie. For years, you have stolen from the masses in order to benefit you and your Boomer friends, and you have the audacity to preach to younger generations after throwing them under the bus. But everything catches up with you eventually, and I'm thrilled I'm the one who gets to do this." She shoved a manilla envelope into Lionel's hands and straightened up to make sure that he was in the view of her lapel camera.

"Oh, yeah," she said, a little embarrassed that she almost forgot to say her line. "I guess crime runs in the family."

Lionel stared at her as if she were a thing.

"I don't get it," he said. "Also, I'm a millennial, not a Boomer."

"You've been served, Francis."

"Lionel."

"You've been served, Lionel."

Lionel nodded at the envelope in his hands.

"What's served?"

"You're getting sued."

"For what?"

"For being a privileged asshole."

"Is that illegal?"

"We're working on it."

"I didn't do anything," said Lionel, not perturbed in the least. "I'm sure we'll figure it out."

"We? Your dad just flew away, and your grandfather's dead."

Lionel looked up from the envelope. He hadn't heard the news. Melanie waited in tense expectation for his reaction.

"I'm sorry to hear that," said Lionel after a loaded pause. Considering the matter further, he added, "I guess that means I'm rich."

Grinning so that his nose crinkled, Lionel tore the manilla envelope open and ripped pages from the subpoena and tossed them into the air. Melanie began a slow walk to her car as the papers floated down around them, and when she was halfway across the lawn, the sprinklers turned on and shot her square in the chest.

"We're in a drought."

"They're automatic."

In her car, she inspected her camera. It was soaked. After a deep breath, she pulled out of the driveway. Her sound system played a synthy, washed-out tune, punctuated with a thumping bass. Checking her side-view mirror, she saw Lionel doing the Milly Rock, a dance trend he saw on YouTube just a week ago. She accelerated, nauseated.

Chapter 3

Socially exhausted from the interaction with Melanie Bobbers, the most excitement he suffered in weeks, Lionel collapsed in front of the computer with an exasperated sigh. Assuming Francis told the truth about not coming back, Lionel had the house to himself for the foreseeable future.

A freshly wrapped joint lay in a crumb-free zone on his desk, and now he could enjoy it in peace. He blew out the smoke so that it spread out against the computer monitor and eddied in the light that shone through the blinds.

Slumping in front of a computer craned his head forward and rounded his weak shoulders, hiding a small chin which drew down farther after years of subvocalizing anxieties he was too timid to share. The few wisps of facial hair sprouting on his chin would not amount to a beard any time soon.

Lionel's last physical took place at a clinic in Manhattan Beach with a muscular blonde man in his 40s named Dr. Wacker, who put specific figures to Lionel's body which he would have preferred to leave as vague details about himself.

"40ᵗʰ percentile for weight."

"Uh-huh."

"4ᵗʰ percentile for height."

"Uh-huh."

"When's the last time you ate a vegetable?"

"It's been a while."

"Hmm."

Dr. Wacker looked into Lionel's ears with an auriscope.

"There is nothing going on in here."

Dr. Wacker had Lionel stick out his tongue and peered in his mouth.

"Nothing in here either."

"What are you looking for?" said Lionel from the back of his throat.

"Anything beyond the pale."

These percentiles put Lionel at 5'4" and 180 pounds. He tried to force these figures out of his mind, but his shape glared back at him in the reflective glass on the storefronts when he trudged back to his Lexus.

YouTube recommended a video called "Christopher Hitchens at his finest." It was a classic, dating back to 2011. Lionel had seen it many times before, but unable to resist, he clicked the video and hit the joint.

Hitchens sat stage left in a debate with the Reverend Al Sharpton. Referring to religion, he said:

> It is their favorite toy, and it will remain so. As Freud said, in The Future of an Illusion, it will remain that way as long as we are afraid of death... which I think is likely to be a long time. Second, I hope I've made it clear that I'm perfectly happy for people to have these toys and to play with them at home and to hug them to themselves and so on and share them with other people who come around and play with their toys. They are not to make me play with these toys. I will not play with the toys. Don't bring the toys to my house...

Lionel snickered lazily, eyes heavy in his high.

A cylindrical ash husk on the end of his joint broke off and landed on his robe. He flicked it onto the floor and scrutinized the mark it left, wincing. A Richard Dawkins video was suggested in the sidebar, and Lionel clicked on it. It was shaping up to be a day of throwbacks. He hit the joint until coughing reflexively exploded out of him, and the computer screen shone brighter, refracted through eye goop. His head throbbed as he recovered, and he had to set the joint down on a shredded Nature Valley granola bar wrapper. His father scolded him about leaving burn marks on his desk.

Lionel's life was so bereft of action that it was difficult to extrapolate any interior life or desire that differentiated him from the rest of the masses slumped in front of a computer screen. But his search history provided a little insight:

ultimate fail compilation
atheist debates christian
nsfw gifs
best of mozart
dinkle's pizza
iraq war footage
faces of death
bob marley playlist
harlem shake
best martial arts moves to win a fight
the god delusion
pick up artist techniques
brazillian jew jitsu
brutal metal playlist
illuminati exposed
street fights
hitchslaps
chiropractor mistakes
the joe rogan experience
funny animal gifs
atmospheric hip hop
dawkins evolution

Although nothing in his search history would raise concern at the NSA, it was notable that it lacked any form of narrative content. Movies used to captivate him as a kid when he enjoyed them unreflectively and when they eventually gave him his sense of self. He grew up in a media landscape that valued portraying his demographic as witty, smooth-talking, but most of all, intelligent. However, this intelligence was not portrayed as a product of hard work or rumination. It was effortless intelligence, intelligence that could be summoned in an instant, intelligence as an essential quality that surmounted all obstacles and bamboozled the lesser minds of adversaries and allies alike. It was not just intelligence Lionel identified with but mostly that it was exceptional, upper margin intelligence, the intelligence of the small subset of people who broke boundaries and rewrote the rules with their breathtaking, innate intelligence.

Lionel saw himself in on-screen prodigies such as Malcolm from *Malcolm in the Middle*, who could deduce the number of dots on the ceiling after a quick glance or derive the answers to complex math equations instantly, drawing exuberant praise from an astounded audience. As he grew older, Lionel identified with Frank Abagnale, played by the preternaturally charming Leonardo DiCaprio in *Catch Me If You Can*, whose intelligence was so off the charts he could slip into the roles of and convincingly pass as a French teacher, an airline pilot, a doctor, and a lawyer, even actually passing the bar. Lionel felt a natural kinship with Will Hunting and assumed that it was his inborn intelligence that made him good, and when his social life took a nosedive in high school, he concluded that no one understood his tragically superior, beautiful mind. He never let the utter lack of evidence deter him from the notion that he was a wunderkind even when his apparently effortless intelligence didn't manifest in any observable phenomena. This was proof to himself that his intelligence was too staggering to be externalized.

His awkward teenage phase coincided with an expanded awareness of how his taste in media branded him, and simply liking something was no longer enough. Artsy films with layered themes and ambiguous meaning became more befitting to his self-conception, and seeing them through the haze of marijuana, which he began to smoke around the time he discovered Tarkovsky, accelerated his devolution from cinephile to atheist.

It was *Stalker* that broke him. Something in the gross sepia and languorous pace took him from transcendent sublime to swearing off stories forever. Marijuana enhanced the film's already loaded portent, and everything teemed with almost unbearable significance, each detail somehow reflecting *Stalker*'s larger statement into a fractal of ubiquitously inscribed meaning, which still remained just out of grasp. It was as though Andrei Tarkovsky whispered through the scenes and waved at Lionel, all the while coyly denying him what he meant.

Significance hovered above Tarkovsky's imagery like smoke until Lionel's favorite atheists came along and blew it away. Even though god was on the top of their shit list, his nonexistence was merely a byproduct of their proper reading of the world which did away with anything but the evidence. They of course were trying to cut down projections of anything supernatural, but their thoughts on religious texts in particular introduced Lionel to a shrewd literary analysis, a lens that distorted everything for him thereafter.

Sam Harris, an atheist he found by listening to *The Joe Rogan Experience*, taught him in a monotone that the parables and stories in the Bible could be interpreted in a number of different ways. Any apparent significance was merely one interpretation or at its worst a projection. Lionel began to consider the meaning in *Stalker* or *Mulholland Drive* or *The Shining* as nothing more than a feeling that the evident imagery conjured within him. Directors know people are going to try to interpret their films, so they must use only the most loaded imagery.

Lionel knew the world didn't have a god much less a director to arrange *mise-en-scène* for interpretation, and as his interest in film died, he dismissed any interpretation of the imagery of his life as a projection that was as delusional as belief in god.

He often fantasized about delivering condescending remarks like his atheist heroes and how his interlocutors would stammer, too flustered to recover. Most of these fantasies remained unrealized, but his mother gave him a few opportunities.

Years ago when Amelia tried to drag him to Easter Mass, an argument exploded between them, and Lionel shared what he had learned, saying in a voice she didn't recognize, "God is a moronic delusion to comfort the stupid." Amelia burst into tears.

She blubbered back to him, "I see Him in the light in your eyes."

Lionel had never heard that argument before, and nothing in his arsenal of stolen retorts would have worked. Although he remained unconvinced, he opined it was time for him to shut up and ponder that maybe she had a life of her own. In a futile gesture, he cleaned his room as she packed her belongings, and Salvatore waited in the driveway, adjusting his ascot in the mirror.

Marijuana tar turned Lionel's sinuses into a swamp, and his eyes regularly seeped goop. To this day, when a floater appeared just off-center of his pupil so that it darted away as he tried to look at it, he playfully thought that his mother had seen something literal on his eyeball. Believers tend to assign fanciful explanations to natural phenomena. A floater crossed from one end of the computer screen to the other.

All the ingredients were laid out for some deep-seated abandonment issues now that both Lionel's parents had run away, or flown in Francis's case, but he regarded their absence with the same indifference he held toward trimmings after a haircut. Unless his psychological complexes, buried from years of smoking weed every day all day, should manifest inappropriately sometime in the future, he was content.

But coinciding with his mother's exit was the feeling that he lost something essential about himself, a little fragment that broke off that would have made him whole. While he pictured it as a missing piece, it was a missing enclosure for him, a place to rest securely, an embrace he longed to disappear into, and after the hole opened in his interior, he tried to find the embrace in the form of roles to slip into, as someone smart and dignified who could trounce bullies in powerful institutions, someone cold and indifferent to the feeble minds of common detractors, someone who didn't feel small when criticized or worthless when everyone around him fit neatly into a community where they were approved of, someone who felt kinship with the greatest minds of their time. This role embraced him. Nestled in this role, he found his warmth.

He couldn't easily give up this embrace. He had already settled in. He identified with it, and he was willing to isolate himself so other people couldn't arouse the tension between himself and who he told himself he was. How awful if he should remove the façade and reveal a skinless body with membranous pulp spilling out.

Richard Dawkins looked into the camera smiling, and the glow of the computer screen started to upstage the information on it. A slight falling sensation emerged that dissociated him from his physical surroundings. In the absence of a strong drive or predicament to occupy his mind, having outsourced all philosophical rumination to the professionals, his vacant interior achieved equilibrium with the outside world. He ceased to exist. It was either ego death by sedentary lifestyle or an experienced abstraction of his place in space-time in which gravity relaxed and let him fall into infinity.

As a man of science, or rather an admirer of men of science, Lionel tried to calm himself with the evidence. *I am Lionel Lancet. I can see objects. Actually, it's the surfaces of the objects, but they're there... At least the ones I'm looking at... There's nothing else.*

But something else, something threatening, loomed beyond the surfaces of the objects in the room. It must have been one of those damned projections lurking around trying to delude him. He thought he had gotten rid of all of those.

Lionel lightly slapped himself in the face.

"I'm right here." Another slap. "Here I am."

But it wasn't his body that felt loosened from the ground. Something from inside felt like it was escaping into the room. He hugged himself as if that would hold it in, but it continued its slow effusive leak. Yearning for something to save him or at least make him an integrated whole, he gathered all of his courage and reached for the joint and lighter. Another hit diffused him further into the space around him.

Chapter 4

No one told Lionel about his grandfather's funeral, and wherever his father flew didn't have cellphone service. Within a week, Lionel fumigated his insides of all signs of intelligent life with back-to-back joints and saturated his stomach with pizza grease. All contact with the outside world had been lost, and gravity influenced his body more than intention. A phone call broke through the lull and startled Lionel so much that he flinched and took a tense moment to collect himself before answering.

"Lionel?"

"Yeah?"

"This is Lee Furnival. I'm your grandfather's attorney."

"He can't come to the phone. He's dead."

"Yes. I'm very sorry for your loss."

"It's a sad thing."

Furnival paused. "There are a few documents I need you to sign concerning his estate."

Lionel perked up. He burned through Francis's fifty rather quickly. "I can come to you. Where are you? I can be there in an hour."

"Let's meet at Santa Monica Pier."

"Sounds good. I'll see you then."

"Wait, let's meet on the far side, closest to the ocean."

"Perfect. Can't wait."

"Hold it. Look for the man in the beige suit."

"Great. I'll see ya then."

"What do you look like so I can find you?"

"I'm a white guy, about 5'4, brown hair."

Lee Furnival was a stressed-out, short, fat man with no hair on the top of his head. He blocked the sun from his eyes with a packet of papers, pushing past tourists, struggling down the walkway that declined sharply from Ocean Ave. A dancer lazily bobbed to music coming out of the speaker strapped around his waist, and a crowd watched him blankly. Families ambled, clumped around dads with kids on their shoulders. Cotton candy stands, hot dog carts, and artist booths that sold custom paintings of names spelled in palm trees, dolphins, and flowers split the waves of passing tourists like wood pilings in the water. Some people stood motionless, looking at nothing in particular, lost in tourist's ennui. The small roller coaster on the far side of the pier chugged along, and the Ferris wheel churned the air, waves of heat squiggling around it.

Furnival scanned the side of the pier that faced the ocean, unable to find Lionel. He leaned against the railing with his head hung until he felt a tap on his shoulder. Lionel stood behind him with a pretzel and slushy.

"This place sucks," said Lionel. "Pretzel?"

He apprehended Lionel, ignoring his offer.

"Face the water," said Furnival.

Lionel obeyed slowly with an uncertain look and rested his pretzel and slushy on the railing.

"You're in a bad way, legally speaking."

"I didn't do anything."

"That's exactly what you need to maintain in court."

"Court?"

"You got a subpoena, didn't you?"

"Yeah, but I'm innocent," said Lionel, with his mouth full of pretzel.

"You still have to show up and say that. What's the court date?"

"I don't know."

"It should be on the subpoena."

"I threw it away."

Furnival said something under his breath, closing his eyes and bowing his head. Lionel reflected for a moment.

"Actually, I threw it into the air, and it blew into the ocean," said Lionel. "But it's gone now."

"What the hell would compel you to do that?"

"It didn't seem very important. I could always get another one."

"Oh, you'll be getting another one. You've got several coming your way."

"It's not even for me. It's for my grandpa."

"According to your grandpa's will, you're listed as the Vice President of his foundation. And since your father renounced his position, you're the president."

"That's impossible."

"It's all in the paperwork."

"Fine. I quit."

"That's your business. I'm staying out of it."

"But aren't you our lawyer?"

"I was your grandpa's lawyer. I don't represent you," said Furnival, looking away and scratching his ear. "But I'd hire a lawyer like yesterday."

"But I'm the president. That makes you my lawyer."

"No."

"Yes."

"No."

"I'm the president," said Lionel, raising his voice.

"Didn't you just quit?"

Lionel opened his mouth to respond, but nothing came out.

Furnival shook his head.

"Whatever," said Lionel. "What about the will? Could I get it in cash?"

"There's no money."

"Is it, like, tied up in stocks?"

"No."

Lionel put his head down on the railing and exhaled through pursed lips. He popped his head up again with an idea.

"So do I get, like, the house or something?"

"No. He left his house and your dad's house to his maid. He arranged for you to live in a pretty swanky villa at the Hotel Bellehaven, if it makes you feel any better. But you'll have to work for them if you want to live there."

Lionel squinted at him.

"This is bullshit," said Lionel.

"You don't have to live there if you don't want to."

"No, all of this. When someone dies, you're supposed to get something like a house or a car... or money. He left me a job?"

"And a villa... and a lawsuit, technically."

Lionel shook his head and looked out at the ocean, taking a frustrated bite of his pretzel.

"I'm just the messenger," said Furnival. "If you want, keep your job–"

"Wake up, Lee. I don't have a job!"

"How do you not have a job?"

"I was selling weed, but I got disenfranchised by legalization." Lionel took a slurp of his slushy.

"A job would be a great thing for you, Lionel. It could give you some direction. Don't you have any goals?"

"I get stressed out easily, so I try to keep my lifestyle kinda low-key." Lionel let out a long sigh, gazing into the horizon. "It's like everything I knew was gone in an instant."

"The loss of a loved one is hard."

"Huh? Oh yeah." With great effort, Lionel asked, "Are the hours flexible?"

"I have no idea," said Furnival, frowning.

"Do they know about the lawsuit?"

"Who?"

"The fucking Hotel Ba... hoosky."

"Bellehaven. I'm not at liberty to discuss what they know."

"Are they going to fire me if they find out?"

"This is California. Everyone's in a lawsuit. Just lie low and work there until you can make your next move. To be honest, I don't care what you do."

"Thanks for the advice," said Lionel in a hollow tone.

"Whoa, this is not legal advice. Actually, can you sign this agreement that this wasn't legal advice? This form too."

"What's this one?"

"It's a Release of All Claims. Just a formality."

Lionel signed a squiggly line on each form and walked away from Furnival.

"You forgot your food."

"It's yours."

A row of sign-wielding Korean Christians began their exit just before Lionel, so it looked as though he joined their procession. Furnival stayed for a while longer to lend credit to his alibi that he trekked out to the pier to watch the waves, which sloshed against the pilings and made a slippery step for the folks who lived underneath.

Chapter 5

The Hotel Bellehaven occupied a small stretch of the beach at the base of the Santa Monica Mountains, south of Malibu. Guests entered from the PCH, driving down a hill toward the ocean past adobe villas and casitas that went for more than $1,000 per night. Coral trees and Magnolias lined the road, and bird of paradise flowers surrounded the executive golf course that spread across the grounds.

The main building of the hotel made a horseshoe around the central circle drive and crept down toward the shore. A man zooming around in a golf cart supervised valet drivers in wicker sun hats who bustled in and out of luxury cars across from a four-tier fountain in front of the entrance.

Inside the lobby, guests in polos and sundresses checked in at a counter beneath an elaborate crystal chandelier and decompressed from their flights at the hotel bar behind curtained French doors that separated it from the rest of the lobby. Hallways with high ceilings branched left and right to suites, conference rooms, and luxury shops that sold purses, makeup, and designer clothing. Past the conference rooms accessible from the north side of the horseshoe, there was an old theater called The Beaumont behind large double doors. No one had performed there in decades.

The far end of the lobby opened out into a limestone deck with loungers and wicker chairs facing the ocean. Beyond the white pavilion that shaded buffet tables below the deck, a path lined with lavatera flowers led to the steakhouse, The Admiral Highbrow, a separate structure.

"You must be Lionel," said Damian, distracted by the registry behind the check-in desk. He stood 6'3", and a light layer of concealer on his face tinged the collar of his white Oxford dress shirt. When he finally looked up, Lionel tensed his shoulders and averted his eyes.

"I was very sad to hear about your grandfather," said Damian. His over-enunciation revealed gleaming white teeth. "You look just like him."

Lionel shrugged.

Damian buttoned his navy suit coat and beckoned Lionel toward the northern hall, walking with a long stride and posture so erect that his shoulders moved. To keep up, Lionel half-jogged, taking in the seashell-embroidered carpet and tables that held vases with glass-blown flowers.

"Is my desk next to a window?" said Lionel. Damian stopped and turned on his heel.

"You don't get a desk. Did you think you were hired for an executive position?" Damian spoke with an upward inflection at the end of his sentences as though he were giving Lionel options to pick from, but rather than doing it airily, his tonal ascent created the impression that Lionel was stupid and needed to be spoken to slowly and clearly.

"Uh... no."

"You'll report to the lobby in the morning so that we can decide what to do with you."

"That's fine. I'd also prefer not to work with people. Or do any cleaning. Or standing for long periods of time."

"You don't get a say. I'm in charge of you, okay?"

"Okay."

"I know you have dreams, but this hotel is my dream, and you work for me."

Twenty years ago, the movie industry lured Damian to Los Angeles from Ohio with dreams of becoming a movie producer, actor, director—any powerful position, really. ICM, one of the top four agencies in the world, hired him as an executive assistant and had him wrapping gifts and ordering fruit baskets for top clients, arranging transportation, booking hotel rooms, and receiving abuse from the monstrous agents whose interest in the film industry came secondary to their sadism. They had been abused themselves and were delighted when it came to be their turn.

Damian would betray not even a wince when the insults flew at him. They were mostly an exercise in catharsis for his bosses, who rarely levied accurate accusations. Confronted by the Executive Agent of Film

Production, Damian had to apologize for apparently looking at the man's wife, projecting deference while rage cooked his insides.

His abusive relationship with his bosses reinforced the sacred ideal of power in him and how it functioned in every relationship: everyone is either the boss or the underling, and if you think you're neither, you're the underling.

While working at ICM, Damian never believed that he was the boss. He barely had a name, and when they did refer to him, he was David, which stuck after no one listened to his repeated attempts to correct them. The hotels he corresponded with got to know him better than any of the agents at ICM, and after getting skipped over for several promotions, mostly because he was never "one of the boys," he let his ambitions for success in the entertainment industry drift toward a career in hospitality. But none of his desire for power or significance dissipated. It got redirected into the Hotel Bellehaven, which was a rather small hole to squeeze it through.

Damian never got to bully anyone at ICM, and now that he had ascended the ranks to become Hotel Manager and Assistant Member of the Board, he relished in sustaining the union between boss and underling from the other side, seething happily.

A conference room with huge swinging mahogany doors let out a horde of people with lanyards around their necks and packets in their hands. According to a poster board presented on a tripod, they were members of the Republican National Convention. Facilitators nodded dutifully beside the conference room doors, smiling at no one in particular as balding men and women in beige pantsuits swarmed into the hall. The crowd congregated densely and moved as a single mass, sweeping Lionel away from Damian toward a catering table with a full breakfast buffet. After a shrug, he started at the bacon, pinching pieces between his fingers and stuffing them in his mouth.

A hand emerged and steered him firmly through a group of sunburned men standing together without speaking. Damian held his grasp and freed Lionel from the crowd.

"We'll need you to stay focused. Yes?"

"Can do," said Lionel, wiping bacon grease on his joggers.

They rounded a corner and entered a hall of guest rooms. Outside the doors lay room service trays with half-eaten sushi rolls, crème brûlée ramekins, lime slices at the bottom of cocktail glasses, and prime rib bones that no one bothered to pick clean. At the end of the hall, a set of double doors led out to the valet's spillover lot, and they passed sports cars and modest rentals alike.

Arriving at a villa beyond the golf course, Damian tried to downplay the presentational air of opening the door to Lionel's swanky new digs. Smiling brightly, Lionel entered and found a full kitchen with a marble-top island in the middle and fresh-cut flowers in a vase on the adjacent countertop. Archways divided the fully furnished living room from the bedroom, and sliding doors beside the bed opened to a brick patio complete with a brownstone fire pit.

Damian pretended he didn't notice Lionel openly beaming.

"We'll need you to change into something more work appropriate," said Damian. As though he had been waiting to say it, he added, "You are an employee here, not a guest."

After Damian left, Lionel spun in a circle like Little Orphan Annie at Daddy Warbucks's mansion. He touched his fingers to the starfish and conch shells on the fireplace mantle in the living room, kicked his feet up on the coffee table in front of the angular modern couch, brewed himself a cup of tea in the kitchen, and dumped it out after one sip. With the bedroom's stereo system blaring "Me OK" by Jeezy, he jumped on the bed which winded him almost immediately.

The Jacuzzi he discovered in the bathroom proved irresistible, and as it filled with water Lionel peeled off his shirt and joggers and flung them on the floor. He entered the hot water with a satisfied sigh. A eucalyptus-scented cube of bath salt dissolved around him, dyeing the water faint green. A fart escaped him, amplified to a hollow bass note beneath the mechanical hum of the jets at his sides.

Pounding sounded on the front door, and Lionel begrudgingly rose and wrapped himself in a complimentary white cotton robe. Trying to conceal his annoyance, he answered the door and found Damian standing on the porch, unamused.

"You're at work right now."

"I thought I was done for the day."

"We need you in the lobby immediately."

He slammed the door shut, and Lionel flinched, a little offended. Damian pounded on the door again, and Lionel opened it. "You are not a guest." He slammed the door shut again, and Lionel flinched again. He could hear Damian's exasperated scoff outside the door.

Still wet, Lionel slipped out of his robe and climbed into the t-shirt and joggers that he flung on the floor.

After jogging, tiring, and resigning himself to walking back to the lobby, Lionel stood up straight with his hands behind his back, catching his breath before succumbing to the urge to lean against the pillar by the check-in counter.

"No leaning," said Damian, emerging from the other side of the pillar. Lionel snapped to attention, startled. "What did I tell you about your clothes? We can't have you dressed like this. Eli Deatherage will be here any day now."

"Is that friend of yours?"

"Hugely important guy. Like, *the* guy," said Damian. "Bazillions of dollars. And yes, we're friends."

"Cool."

"He produced *Carriers of the Cosmos*."

"Is that related to Carl Sagan?"

"It's, like, the biggest movie ever."

Damian informed Lionel that Eli Deatherage, along with everyone in the Deatherage family, was famous, chic, and used to special treatment. Eli's wife Susan Deatherage ran an internationally renowned foundation with dozens of charities under its umbrella. Jade (rhymes with bad) Deatherage, their eldest son, starred in the show *Jade Attitude* on Comedy Central. Violet Deatherage, their eldest daughter, led a fashion line called *Drab* that she started at 19. Macheck Deatherage, their second son, hosted a cooking show on the Food Network called *Shuck Me Roughly*. Even Burt, the toddler, had an Instagram account with 2 million followers.

"And I think they have another daughter."

"What does she do?"

"I don't know. There are, like, twelve of them," said Damian. "Eli is *the* guy. If he likes you, you get catapulted to the top of the industry."

"I'm not trying to be in the industry."

"I'm not talking about you." Damian patted the part in his hair. "It's extra crucial that he doesn't see you lying around playing with yourself."

"I wasn't playing with myself."

"So I'm going to need you not to talk back either. That makes me look bad."

"But—"

"Lionel, come here." Damian put his hand on Lionel's shoulder, which he received tensely. "What's the matter with you? You're mopey and out of it. Your clothes are all fucked up and covered in cum."

"That's toothpaste." Lionel inspected his joggers. It was actually gunk he scraped from his tooth with his thumbnail.

"You need to put more effort into your appearance. And your hair? What's the deal? This is a luxury resort hotel, not a homeless camp."

Lionel gave a bored, passive face.

"Say something."

"So it's all about appearances, huh?"

"Yeah." Damian widened his eyes. "That's what I just said."

Lionel subscribed to the popular pseudoscience that assigned Greek letter classifications to rank men in a hierarchy. Of course, he considered his intelligence to be vastly superior to others,' but standing 5'4" with a proclivity to clam up in confrontations with other men, he suffered no delusion that he was an "alpha." Damian towered over him and indulged in one of the many privileges that Lionel perceived tall men were granted: the permission to share negative emotions. He assumed that any confrontation of his own would be invalidated out of hand as a fraudulent attempt at passing as a higher rank on the hierarchy.

"I just don't understand why you wouldn't want to meet a famous producer," said Damian, frowning.

"I'm not really a film guy."

"What, you think he's gonna write a part for you? He only works with people with experience in the industry." Damian gazed past Lionel for a moment. "But from now on, you're going to be presentable. Right?"

"Okay."

"Great," said Damian, clapping his hands. "There are rules that keep the hotel in good shape, so we can deliver excellent service and make money. That's the main idea. No good service, no guests, no money. It can seem daunting, but after you learn the rules it can be invigorating, fun... and cool!

"The general rule for excellence is the rule of surfaces. Look around you. The entire world is big and scary, but we can break it down into smaller pieces and know every surface of every piece. So what I need you to do..." Lionel stiffened, sensing that work was being delegated. "...is to take this rag..." Damian withdrew a rag with an unnecessary flourish. "...and this spray bottle..." He withdrew a bottle of cleaner that seemed too large to have fit within his coat. "... and go through every surface on the inside and outside of the hotel, and make sure it's clean enough to eat off of." Damian unloaded everything into Lionel's arms.

Blood throttled in Lionel's veins as the immensity of the task that lay before him sank in. The variety of surfaces there were in the lobby alone was staggering—every side of every table, inside drawers, pillars that reached to the ceiling, the inside and outside of the register, the tops and bottoms of all rugs, umbrella holders, coat racks, windows, walls, floors, door handles, hinges, baggage carts, bar stools, ornamental seashells, shelving units, guard rails... And what about the people? Surely, they were a complex of surfaces as well. Lionel blinked back tears.

"Every surface?" said Lionel.

"*Every* surface."

"Isn't that impossible? That guest is holding a basketball. One of the surfaces is on the inside."

"Then, fill an air pump with soapy water, pump it in, and squeeze it out."

"I just got really hot."

Sweat dripped into Lionel's eyes, and his shirt, which was already damp, started to cling to his lower back. Another dissociative lapse was coming, in which that mysterious something inside of him shifted and made plans to escape into the room. A ripple stirred his surroundings like something beyond surfaces was rustling about, and his heartbeat rang into every nerve like a hysterical alarm. Each throb of his heart rolled through him and thrummed at the spot in his head where he felt he resided, loosening it and opening it and spreading it all over the hotel lobby. A grave sadness met him there.

"What are you doing?" Damian recoiled from him.

Lionel heard him, but it was just one of almost infinite phenomena that subsumed him, including throaty corporate voices, a phantasmagoria of checkered collared shirts and pantsuits, enormous cellphones clipped to leather belts. Throughout this ego erasure, Lionel's mouth hung open, and he drooled. The air entered his lungs warm and stagnant like he was breathing from a paper bag. Something like survival instincts kicked in, and before he knew what he was doing, he tore off his shirt and crouched on all fours, clinging to the ground to remind himself he was still embodied.

Damian's face couldn't decide between horror and disgust. Guests' chatter into cell phones and conference attendees' vague plans to keep in touch stopped all at once, and everyone stared at Lionel. Damian gestured for a lower rank to usher him away, and he announced to the room, "Nothing to worry about." But he could not shake what he witnessed.

Later that day, he appeared at the door of Lionel's villa and graciously avoided any mention of the incident, but his limited eye contact and polite distance indicated that it was still fresh in his mind.

"You're being demoted."

"Will there be more money?"

"No. *De*moted. That's not how that works. Also, did you eat bacon from the buffet? They count the bacon, you know."

"No."

"I would have loved to start out with my grandfather on the board of directors. I had no connections, no experience, and a fear of resorts. But that didn't prevent me from ascending the ranks—bellboy to Luggage Manager to Chief Representative of Guest Services to Hotel Manager and Assistant Member of the Board. All without losing sight of my film career."

"Film career?"

"I've got a few projects in escrow," said Damian, feigning nonchalance. "And a feminist Christmas story that's like this close. Besides, I'm producing hotel experiences now. It's the same."

Lionel saw desperation and pain beneath the concealer on Damian's serious face and was surprised to find him endearing in spite of their already strained working relationship. But Lionel suppressed this feeling and dismissed it as a random thought.

"So what's my new job?"

"You'll be in the lobby."

"Doing what?"

"Attending," said Damian. "You'll be a lobby attendant."

"So I have to sit there and kiss people's asses? And point like this," said Lionel, gesturing with his palm up, "instead of like this?" He pointed his index finger.

Damian flinched. "Don't point that at me. You'll stand and greet guests and act like a civilized person who wears nice clothes without wrinkles and bathes daily and gets regular haircuts."

"So what do I do then? Just sit there?"

"You'll stand there and be engaging and charming and fun."

"So I've got to sit there and talk to people?"

"Everyone will be tired from traveling. You just smile and comment on traffic and direct them to the front desk." Damian caught himself leaning forward with his head low, which gave him a double chin. He straightened his posture and said, "And you'll be standing."

Chapter 6

Eli Deatherage first crossed Art Lancet's path after the installation of a controversial lawn ornament in Art's front lawn led to a board of review at the Society for Historical Homes. The ornament in question was a giant statue of the Hindu goddess Kali, which tested the conservative sensibilities of Palos Verdes. The ranch's status as a historical landmark was called into question by the sitting chairman at the time, Max Rabier, who tried to sustain the momentum he gathered from exaggerating his disgust at the "wretched addition" to the "formerly tasteful house."

"I'm allowed to decorate my lawn how I see fit," said Art.

"But with such... imagery?" At forty-eight, Max Rabier was the youngest chairman in the SHH's history. His hair went gray at the temples, which meant he stopped having to dye it that way in vying to be a silver fox since his early 30s, but Art always viewed him as too much of a boy scout to lead the society with any real gravitas.

Art shouted into Max's cute little face, "It's art! You are the only one who thinks it's offensive. Besides, it's on my property. Nothing about it changes the historic value of the house."

"Historical value," said Max. "And the committee has to uphold the standards for historical homes, or else the designation means absolutely nothing."

"I'm not taking it down, and that's the end of it."

"The SHH will never tolerate unapproved statues, let alone a gross spider woman holding a severed head."

"You are clueless, Max."

"It's obscene and a blight on our reputation. I would also like to draw the society's attention to this photo." Max wheeled a projector out and plugged his laptop into it. The photo of Art's ranch appeared on the wall.

"So what?" said Art.

"Allow me to zoom in." Max zoomed in on one of the shutters on the window outside of the master bedroom, and Art froze.

"Now, I'm no expert. Ah, who am I kidding? Yes I am. But I didn't know that they made shutters like that in the 1950s. Mr. Lancet, will you please read into the record what that little logo says?"

"There's no record being taken."

"How about you read it so everyone can hear."

"Roof Co."

"A little louder?"

"Roof Co! Pedantic little bastard."

"There's no need for that," said Max. "Now, people of the Society for Historical Homes: Roof Co. is a corporation that didn't start mass-producing tasteless house fixtures like these until the 1980s." Art buried his face in his hands. "I'm proposing the removal of Mr. Lancet's home from the Society for Historical Homes registry. All in favor?"

Resounding "I"s haunted Art's sleep. He and Constance moved to the Hotel Bellehaven so that the ranch might be properly renovated and decorated with close oversight from the Society for Historical Homes, even though he started referring to the group as the Society for Hysterical Homes, which Constance roundly ignored. After failed negotiations, Art agreed to sell the Kali statue. The highest bidder was Eli Deatherage, whose cream-colored French revival mansion in Holmby Hills enjoyed the city of Los Angeles's lax regulations regarding lawn ornaments. Their mutual interest in Eastern religions led to a friendship and eventually a business partnership that would last until Art's death. It was Art who talked Eli into investing in the Hotel Bellehaven and his foundation, the Fiduciary Royalties Association for United Donors.

Eli was reluctant. He had many other irons in the fire financially speaking, but he would be humiliated if even one of them went cold. Even marginal losses in his portfolio threatened to ruin his image as the provider for his family. A bad year could relocate their annual trip to France to some fledgling resort in Florida. But Art won him over with spirituality, saying, "It is a weak investor who invests with his ego."

Eli's investment in the hotel panned out well for the most part. Conferences of various kinds kept the Hotel Bellehaven rich, filling the guest registry with lanyard-wearing professionals who were shipped in from corporate branches all over the world on their company's dime as a top-earners reward. With their rooms paid for, attendees spent more on the spa amenities, the Admiral Highbrow steakhouse, and the excursions department. These conferences generated millions of dollars for the hotel until Art's flamboyant spirituality caught the attention of one Melanie Bobbers.

Art hosted an annual retreat at the hotel, which cost attendees $5,000 for a tier-one ticket, $8,000 for tier-two, and a hefty $15,000 for tier-three. Hundreds were happy to attend on tier-one, where they were treated to rooms, small group meditation instruction, and spots in the conference hall for the Spirituality and Business lecture panel, led by Art. Still more signed up for tier-two, which added complimentary spa amenities, room service, and a Sanskrit mantra customized to the participant's skull shape, determined by none other than Carl Das, a monk who went by Carl Lewandowski to the folks who knew him when he sold insurance. Tier-three, however, capped enrollment at twenty people and required a personal invitation from Art himself. It didn't appear in the promotional brochures that got sent out in advance of the retreat.

Melanie would never deign to purchase a ticket, but she found out about the retreat by chance while out on a day trip, hiking the public access trail that led behind the hotel, where she came upon a woman who collapsed on the ground. The woman's dilated pupils seemed to see things that Melanie could not.

"I'm calling an ambulance," said Melanie.

A devilish grin appeared on the woman's face, and she asked, "Why? Is somebody hurt?"

"Are you okay?"

"Just communing with the creator of the universe. She's nice."

"What did you take?"

"It tasted like paint."

"Did you take it voluntarily?" The woman seemed distracted with something floating in front of her face like she was following an invisible fly. "Did you take the drug yourself or did someone give it to you?"

"I'm tier-three, thank you very much."

Melanie observed her. "Are you with someone or are you out here alone?"

"All of us are in it together. Unless of course you're tier-one or two," said the woman, erupting in laughter. Suddenly grave, she said, "Oh no. Are you tier-one or two?"

"I'm not tier anything."

"You have to meet Art. He'll sign you up."

"Is he the one who gave you whatever you took?"

"He poured it. I drank it." She giggled.

"That sick fuck."

"Honey, he's a good man."

"I've heard enough."

Melanie was after him ever since, broadening her skill set to become a sleuth. After an extensive investigation into Art's personal and professional history, she made a horrifying discovery: he was a rich white man who appropriated other cultures for personal gain. She also suspected that he was a rapist, but she had not yet found the smoking gun. A five-part, documentary-style hit piece on her vlawg exposed the suspicious financing of his foundation, and ticket holders of all tiers demanded refunds, effectively canceling the conference. The Hotel Bellehaven had been in the red ever since.

Art said that that was just the ebb and flow of life, but Eli didn't see it that way. Funding a movie, even one that loses money, still makes for a good brag. But losing money on a hotel is just a failed investment. Art had gone and died before Eli had a chance to retaliate for getting him involved, and the board pleaded that he summon his financial muses to save the doomed hotel. Stoically masking his panic, he brought the whole family to the Hotel Bellehaven on a supposed vacation, certain he could slip away to urgent meetings and take furtive phone calls on the beach. But there was still the problem of his involvement in Art's corrupt foundation. For that, he would have to get creative.

Lionel smiled weakly at guests who entered the lobby, tensing at their approach, and breaking eye contact immediately so they would pass him to attend to their booking at the front desk. Every so often, a guest would take his hollow welcome personally and square up with him for a moment to explore what he considered a surface-level interaction that demanded no further investigation. In these moments, Lionel strained to maintain the cheerfulness that made the guest talk to him in the first place, and when a grimace surfaced on his gloomy, droopy face, the guest would leave let down, having been caught on the receiving end of such an immediate reversal from invitation to dismissal.

The rest of his life stretched out before him, trapping him in eternal attendance of the lobby, which seemed to be getting on just fine without him. Men and women drifted through toward destinations unknown to him, and kids occupied themselves, dangling off their parents and furniture, all with the whimsy of vacation. Someone was speaking loudly about the sushi at Sugarfish, expressing their disapproval that their friend went to the wrong spot, and the friend protested that they did in fact go to Sugarfish, which was met with the accusation they ordered the wrong dish. Lionel bristled at each elongated, Californian o in "wrong." The surrounding objects remained motionless, but he wouldn't put it past them to let out whatever they'd been holding back.

The din of the hotel lobby and rhythmic tide behind him blended into white noise that lulled him into a respite from the outside world where snapshots of the present moment pursued separate timelines and meshed their contents with his fantasies—the hotel guests moving slowly to music, crowding around him, looking at each other, merging into a single body with many heads but one muffled voice that punctuated the music with some indecipherable three-syllable word, trying to rouse him from his waking sleep to tell him something.

"Lionel," said Damian.

"Huh?"

A small crowd formed around him, Damian at the front, his performative smile wide around his whitened teeth. Behind him stood a family to whom Damian apologized. They didn't react.

"This is the Deatherage family." Damian turned bright and welcoming around Eli, who didn't give him a second glance.

Jade had the same dark, round eyes as his father and seemed to have also inherited disregard for how he came off to people. Machek was shorter and plumper, and he carried himself with notable poise. Violet had cold blue eyes and held her mouth open, studying Lionel. Fussing in her arms was Burt, who shared the same distinguished air as the rest of them, even as a toddler. He spotted the cookies on the front desk and trained his eyes on them.

Susan Deatherage stood in the center of the pack, and after Lionel fully appraised the scene, he saw that each member of the family was connected to her through various degrees of bodily separation. Burt clasped her finger. Jade leaned against her lovingly without stopping his disdainfully staring at Lionel. Machek's perfect posture made him appear separate at first, but his left love handle spilled over his waistline, grazing Violet's elbow. Eli Deatherage had his hand on Susan's back as he spoke into his phone.

While the rest of the family either ignored Lionel or looked at him as if he were a thing, Susan gazed at him with eyebrows raised in polite expectation. She was unperturbed by the various connections she sustained, as though she radiated life easily and each of her family members depended on her for vitality. Lionel felt unprotected and useless next to them as though their group dynamic hung him out over a wide canyon.

Baggage boys and events staff stole glances at them, and guests looked up from their tablets and excitedly exchanged whispers. It was apparent just in the way they carried themselves that they were used to being a spectacle, and they wore it well, no faux modesty nor relishing in the attention. Everyone gravitated toward them, desperate to be near them, to please them, to absorb their energy, and they didn't seem to notice.

The only one immune to their aura was Lionel, who looked back at them blankly, not recognizing any of them.

"Please take the Deatherages to their suite," said Damian. Lowering his voice, he added, "Close your mouth."

Lionel snapped to attention and rushed away from the front desk in order to lead them, but he froze when he encountered another Deatherage behind the clump—Tomiina Deatherage, who had green eyes and a beret set on top of her bob haircut that was so free of any stray strands of hair that it looked like it was set on her head in one piece like Lego hair. She stood separate from her family.

Seeing the hidden Deatherage daughter struck Lionel with déjà vu. He might have seen her in a movie trailer or an ad somewhere online, but the familiarity of her face was uncanny, transforming their encounter into an extremely grave matter for him. He willed his legs to continue their pace, but they ignored him, keeping him planted.

The gawkers around them thought they were witnessing a movie-worthy meet cute, but for Lionel, it was something else entirely. Some echo of eternity resonated between them and expanded inside him as a feeling of doom. She apprehended him calmly. Where had he seen her before? Perhaps in another life.

Ringing filled his ears, and his heart swelled and pulsed in his chest, reverberating a field around him that rattled the chandeliers and vibrated through the dried sea creatures within their decorative bowls. Everyone cowered at the shaking in the room. From beyond the appearances of the objects in his surroundings, something pressed itself toward him and dragged the outlines of everything in a slow, fluid stroke. His interior shook as if a deep bass note sounded in his core and slowed so that every phase of the sound wave rocked him back and forth.

Falling to his knees then on his side, Lionel clawed at his collar, and Damian crouched down, stopping him from tearing off his shirt again.

"Just a tremor. Nothing to worry about," Damian announced to the room as the shaking subsided. He stood and pulled at the hem of his suit coat, smiling apologetically at the Deatherages. Nervous laughter and sighs of relief came out intermittently before everyone noticed Lionel, who was the only one knocked to the ground.

"I'm so sorry about him. He does not represent the hotel."

Lionel shifted to lie on his back, and after a deep breath, he sat up. Tomiina offered him a hand, and he accepted it, rising to a knee and then to his feet.

"I'll be sure that this never happens again." Damian turned to the Deatherages for approval.

"Stop," said Tomiina. "He's fine."

"As long as you're not uncomfortable with... the way he is," said Damian.

"Could you back up, please?" said Tomiina.

Damian, tight-mouthed, took a dutiful step backward.

Tomiina brought a hand to Lionel's cheek, and a warm sensation spiraled out of the points where her hand met his skin, eroding tension he didn't know he'd been carrying.

"I'm joking," said Damian with great effort. "Lionel is a great employee. But trust me, you'll get sick of him." He tried to laugh, but no one joined him.

"I don't want to stand here all day," said Eli.

"Take them to suite 1800, Lionel." Damian handed him the card keys. Being trusted with the most important guests at the hotel seemed far beyond Lionel's capability, especially as he was still winded from his lapse, but he stood up straight and beckoned them, accidentally making awkward eye contact with Jade, who narrowed his eyes. Instantly writing someone off must be a privilege afforded to celebrities, Lionel decided, fashioning his upbringing in Palos Verdes as humble roots he best not forget. Should he ever happen into fame, he promised himself then and there to be kind to even the lowliest lobby attendant.

As Lionel led the Deatherages to their suite, a grin spread across his face, and ticklish warmth smoldered in his abdomen. The high from the joint he smoked that morning wore off, but he felt encapsulated by an unfamiliar giddy sensation.

As the Deatherages filed into their suite, Tomiina stopped outside the door.

"I'm Tomiina."

"Lionel." He looked at her, unsure of what to do. She smiled, and he took that as permission to smile back. After an extended moment in which neither of them said a thing, Tomiina left him standing in the doorway.

Lionel gazed into their suite a little too long, and Jade shut the door in his face. The door's percussive slam shook Lionel, but his smile returned before long. He drifted through the hallway as though borne aloft by the adrenal throb that Tomiina induced by simply looking at him. The Deatherage's suite fixed itself in his awareness, and as he made his way back to the lobby, he could orient himself in relation to that last moment he saw her as if its point in spacetime radiated outward.

Chapter 7

"I'm demoting you again."

Lionel nodded in complete agreement, having returned to the lobby with that very expectation. It was only his second day, but the burden of work weighed on him with existential fatigue that spread his attention into a scattershot, landing anywhere from the raw adrenal tenderness in his lungs to the ache haloing his head. If luck would have it, his next role would keep him away from human interactions so he could dissociate and tear off his shirt in peace. Perhaps a seated position in a closed filing room full of papers that were already filed would suit him. There, he could keep watch for movement beyond the material plane and hold everything in place if necessary.

"Didn't I tell you to buy new clothes?"

"I don't know."

"Buy new clothes. Immediately. Also a word of advice: close your mouth. You're gaping like a bass." The lobby cleared out after the Deatherages left, so Damian was free to abandon professional decorum, reaching toward Lionel's face and closing his mouth for him.

Lionel recoiled with his shoulders up to his ears. Any attempt at standing up for himself would certainly be met with mockery, so he settled for presenting harmlessness, convinced his passivity was something like compassionate grace gifted to the world—one mouth fewer spraying irrationality and venom. The feeling of Damian's hand remained on his chin.

"I need you to go notarize this document in Santa Monica."

Out in the parking lot, Lionel backed up his Lexus too fast and slammed on the breaks inches short of a fire hydrant. The resulting whiplash struck him as another injustice that threatened to break him. He would need to smoke it out later in the Jacuzzi. Damian supervised his exit from the lobby entrance, shaking his head.

Lionel fought traffic and arrived at a notary office that hadn't been renovated since the '80s. Dim light through the entryway's wall of wavy glass block windows lit the interior. He absorbed the nostalgia of the faded corporate aesthetic through a fantasy of working there, contained in an era already spoken for, driving home to Tomiina, who would appreciate his willingness to work in spite of her wealth. A man in a gray suit scanned the papers that Lionel handed over the white Formica countertop of the front desk that had taken on a dingy yellow.

"I need verbal acknowledgment that everything in this Transfer of Assets is correct."

"Uh-huh."

The man looked up at Lionel, displeased.

"Yes, sir. Sir, yes, sir."

"Please sign here."

Lionel signed, and the man stamped the notary seal with the date next to it at the bottom of the document and signed his name.

"Have a nice day."

"That's it?"

The man ironically did a sign of the cross over the document. "How's that?"

"I had to drive all the way here for a stamp? Unbelievable."

Back at the hotel, Lionel crossed the circle drive toward the lobby, and Damian emerged from the entrance to snatch the notarized document away from him. Upon seeing the signature and stamp, Damian's face lit up. In spite of succeeding at his task, Lionel felt uneasy standing in Damian's vicinity and turned his feet toward his villa in a timid request to be dismissed.

"Lovely Lionel. Does anyone ever call you that?"

"...no."

"I have another delivery for you to make, Lovely Lionel."

"Cool."

"*Cool,*" mocked Damian, slouching. "*I'm Lionel. Whatever. I don't care.*" Damian waited for some response from Lionel, who already learned to harden around him. "The guests want to see happy faces during their stay. They have terrible lives in the Midwest, and they work the whole year to be here for a few days." Damian smiled ostentatiously. "Give it a try."

Lionel pretended to not understand. Damian closed the space between them, tucked the document under his arm so he could grab the sides of Lionel's face and press the edges of his mouth up with his thumbs. Lionel's eyes widened like a scared dog's.

"Lovely Lionel."

Lionel shook Damian off of him and didn't break eye contact in the moment after when it was his turn to do anything at all. The day was already an onslaught of requirements, demanding that he acknowledge and engage with phenomena that served only to drain him. No countermove occurred to him. Besides, any retaliation would only provoke Damian further.

Lionel backed away and turned onto a footpath that led toward his villa. He stepped into the grass, oblivious, and tramped on the Hotel Bellehaven's freshly stamped seal—a circle divided into even quarters with seagulls flying about, a bundle of flowers, the main structure of the hotel, and a mystical smokey plume in front of stars. A sign driven into the ground on a wooden stake said "Keep Off the Grass."

"Lionel! Can't you read?"

"It's the ground. We're supposed to walk on it."

Damian stomped over to him and stopped just shy of the grass.

"That seal represents everything we work for."

"Looks like a circle with birds on it."

"It stands for something."

"What is it with you and stamps?"

"Come here," said Damian. Lionel slowly crossed so that Damian could shout in his face more directly. Cologne intermingled with the air Lionel inhaled. "You see all of this? The grounds? The golf course? The goddamn hotel itself? All of this wasn't an accident. It didn't just show up here one day. Everything had to be put here carefully. Every stone in that wall had to be placed. Every picture had to be hung. Every blade of grass had to be planted by someone."

"You planted the grass seeds one by one?"

"Of course not—"

"Wouldn't it be faster to just spread a bunch of seeds at once?"

"Obviously. I'm making a point," said Damian, adjusting the waist of his blazer. "That isn't just a stamp. It's a stamp of the Hotel Bellehaven's seal, and it contains all of its history and its promise to give guests a five-star experience. And the work that *some of us* do is in that seal. You will respect it."

"It's literally just paint on the ground."

"I need you to go through the grass and comb out your footprints." Lionel didn't budge. "Right now."

"You can't even see where I stepped."

"You need to learn respect for—"

"For your authority?"

"No. Actually, yes. For my authority. My authority runs the hotel."

"Looks like it's doing fine on its own."

They shared a silent beat. Damian pointed at the ground.

Lionel gazed into the mountains with his hands on his hips. Something in the bush-dotted peaks, absent of any human structures, called to him. Situated in one of the valleys, he could will out of existence anything that tried to suck his energy, slowly disappearing into the landscape to remain inert for thousands of years. But from his current vantage point, the only ground available to him was stamped with a corporate design, and Lionel had no evidence that he could be anything outside of the role it required of him. He knelt and combed his hands through the grass.

"Pull that weed right there," said Damian, his head tilting higher. "Very good. This place is turning into a fucking jungle."

Once Lionel finished, Damian was quick to assign him his next task: delivering a dozen cardboard boxes to 448 Hillcrest Drive. Or was it 446 Hillcrest Drive? Under normal circumstances, Lionel would have stayed sharp with a few joints by this time of day, but his new job changed the regularity of his self-medication, and his body was still adjusting. Verifying the address with Damian might have incited further abuse, so he decided it was 448 Hillcrest Drive after all. He parked his Lexus in the circle drive next to the fountain, and a bellboy helped load the boxes into the trunk. Before Lionel drove away, Damian peered into the driver's side window. "I'm going out of town for a while, so I need you to be on good behavior. Please don't do anything weird. You can take off work in fact."

"Really?"

"It's just a couple of days. Go explore. Go to Joshua Tree or New York."

Lionel sped away and felt the weight of Damian's authority dissipate. Rolling down the windows, he looked away from the road, but something moved in his periphery, and he slammed on the brakes to avoid killing an octogenarian who walked into the main drive, crossing to the executive golf course. Lionel waved apologetically. The old golfer looked more offended than afraid.

At the top of the main drive, Lionel floored the gas pedal into the turn, fishtailing as he roared south on the PCH. Traffic became dense where The 1 turned into The 10, and his joyride settled into a slow roll. Irritated breath escaped his nostrils. There were cars in front of him as far as he could see. Even miles away from Damian, Lionel was trapped. His thoughts drifted to Tomiina and how any life with her would be impossible as long as he worked at the Hotel Bellehaven.

Beneath the overpass, bird's nests held on in crevices where the concrete supports met the beams above. Stains from road sediment and drainage spread out wide like auras on the sloped walls. Lionel closed his nasal passage with the back of his tongue and soft palate to block the smell of body soil and urine. Homeless people sauntered about and sat on five-gallon buckets in front of tents and shopping carts full of plastic bags and empty bottles. A woman with gray hair sat in a recliner by a dilapidated vanity. A man with grocery bags on his feet coughed productively, and another man lay on the ground, motionless, with his right eye missing along with a significant portion of flesh around it. The wound was a pulpy red-yellow. He was dead as far as Lionel could tell.

Lionel shrank in his seat. The pain and abjection among the small gathering were too much for him to bear, and as cars in front of him started to move, he forced the image from his mind, dismissing it as nothing more than a passing sight.

At 448 Hillcrest Drive, Tony Motion lay sulking in bed. Earlier that day while shooting a threesome in a room full of gilded-frame mirrors so that every cleft of breast and thrusting pelvis reflected from all angles, Tony noticed his own despondent face. He shifted his glance elsewhere, but another mirror reflected his tired eyes looking sadly through his dreadlocks.

Tony was a short, black man in a loose-fitting orange silk shirt with matching pants. He hadn't produced a hit since *Agile Twinks III,* a stunt-heavy pornographic blockbuster that fulfilled its promise to somersault over, gainer past, and juke out all adult films that came before it. Journalists, activists, and paid subscribers alike adored the film's acrobatic sexual maneuvers and gymnastic stunts, and more money rolled in than he could keep track of. But when he accepted his AVN award for Best Film, he felt detached. He knew it would be his biggest production and his last great idea.

The pitches that used to rouse celebration in production meetings were gone. Everyone became interested in their nails or the birds flying past the window. Tony's pornographic sitcom *Balls in the Family* "could work." *Full Metal Jack Off* "would be interesting." But there was a sense among his production team that they were trying to keep something alive past its expiration.

Tony continued to wake up five days a week only to avoid performers' requests for direction. Crew members learned not to bother him at all. Anyone who managed to corner him got an exasperated sigh.

A dark mood descended on him accompanied by the feeling that he had passed into a new dimension where nothing existed beyond the reflections in the mirrors and the bodies in the room. He took a deep breath to calm himself in light of the sense of doom that hung over him along with the certainty that death would be the end. No higher order cradled the moment, and even time didn't continue in any reliable way. There was only space and the objects in it. It was only a matter of luck that his body hadn't been destroyed in a car accident or by an earthquake or a meteorite colliding on a perfect trajectory with his skull.

A cold sweat condensed on his palms, and his core trembled. It occurred to him that at death he'd feel the urge to grasp onto something to stop himself from slipping away, but there would be no away to arrive at and nothing to hold onto that would prevent his exit. Just a dissipation into nothing.

Evidence of the cafeteria-style servings of L.A.'s spiritual offerings rested on his mantle: amethyst crystals, a wooden Buddha figure, a crucifix, a little unburned palo santo. Dabbling allowed for some notion of an afterlife, but he believed in it the same way he believed in Mt. Kilimanjaro or the bubonic plague: a matter of fact that he had no experience with.

Death's promise to erase him cast a new light on his life. He dreamed of being an artist, an auteur, but porn paid the bills, and he settled. He bargained that film had been a pipe dream, hubris disguised as artistic ambition. All his sweeping statements about "movies nowadays" and the '70s as the sweet spot for "real film" made him sound like an old-head anyway. Weren't movies just escapism? He had a good group of friends and lovers and *Agile Twinks III,* and the afterlife would compensate him for anything else that didn't pan out.

Scored with the sound of sex, the finality of death rang through him, exposing all his negotiations as the lies that they were. It was like murky water became still, and the silt settled beneath. Eternity wasn't a consolation prize for his failure. And his supposed detour into the porn industry was no different than "movies nowadays:" all body and no soul.

Faking heartburn, he told the women to keep going without him. Tears came before he made it up the stairs.

Was there enough time left to commit to his dreams without the safety net of heaven? What story did he even have to tell? Collapsing on his bed, he prayed that whatever his story was, it would be his life's work, that it wouldn't be escapism, that it would be the ultimate commitment to this life. And as his body reminded him once more that there was nothing but the material world, he prayed that his story would prove there was a soul inside of him that could escape.

After pulling into the driveway at 448 Hillcrest Drive, Lionel stopped in front of a wrought-iron gate with the initials TM in gothic lettering at the center. A trellised arcade covered in ivy extended on the other side blocking the view of the house. Lionel pushed the button on a callbox at the gate. After a *beep,* the gate parted at the center, and Lionel drove under the arcade and ascended a broad hillside with evenly spaced Jacarandas and

Coral trees. A tiered granite fountain at the center of the lawn cascaded into a circular coy pond, and a small labyrinth of hedges surrounded it. Several film studio trucks were parked in parallel on a shipping paddock to the right of the house.

As Lionel brought his car to a stop in front of the steps that led to the doorway, Marcus, a tall man in a red tracksuit, came out.

"What's this about?" said Marcus.

"No clue," said Lionel. "I'm just the messenger."

"What's the message?"

"Err, I'm just the delivery guy."

With his dreadlocks hanging over his face, Tony Motion appeared in the doorway. He wrapped himself in a robe that sported the initials TM. A teal Macaw with an orange breast flapped onto his shoulder and raised its wings proudly.

"Delivery," said Lionel. "Boxes."

Tony said nothing. He wiped his face with his hand. Lionel nodded and shoved his hands in his pockets.

"Am I getting sued?" said Tony. His voice was small and lifeless.

"I don't know."

Tony looked disappointed in that answer. "All right. Load it in. Let's take twenty. I'm getting sued."

Lionel heaved the first box out of the trunk and up the stairs before letting it drop in the entryway of the house. Before going back for the second, he bent over with his hands on his knees, gasping for air. Marcus unloaded the rest, and Lionel gave an appreciative wave.

In the sitting room next to the entryway, women lounged in various states of undress. They flipped through magazines and checked their hair and makeup in compact mirrors. One of them was tuning a ukulele. Blushing, Lionel pretended to adjust the lids on the boxes as his eyes wandered toward the sitting room. No amount of clenching and moving his mouth could stifle the smirk that settled there. Marcus ushered him out and shut the door behind him. The lock turned from inside with a click. Lionel scoffed in offense. Returning to the car, he peered over his shoulder for a peek through the window. The curtains drew closed. He didn't expect to be invited to stay, but it disappointed him that no one tried to make more of the interaction. He lit a joint he started the day before and got in his car.

Chapter 8

The sun reflected off the Hotel Bellehaven's southern-facing windows and cast its soft gold on the grounds. The taller chaparral bushes between the hotel and beach rustled in the warm breeze coming in. Lionel lay reclined in a lounge chair beside a reflecting pool, staring out over the ocean, raising a glass of chilled wine to his lips. The sommelier left her cart unattended.

To the south, Lionel could see all the way to Santa Monica Pier. Figures with their wetsuits half peeled off lay spread out on beach towels, and a few in swimsuits braved the cold and waded out until the water was up to their waists. Dogs and their owners trotted along the beach path. Tomiina was nowhere to be found.

Lionel rose and returned to the lobby, and there she stood in a floral sarong, black one-piece swimsuit, and floppy sun hat. Her eyes found his as though she expected his entrance.

A full-body shiver took hold of him. Tomiina's forward-grown face with the pleasant curve of her nose and elegant little chin aligned with a stencil that resided somewhere deep in his subconscious. Welling energy awakened within him, and he had to lean against a pillar to keep from falling over. A bellboy wheeled a luggage cart between the two of them, and Lionel used this as an opportunity to run away.

As if on their own, his legs piloted him out of the lobby, down the hallway, past the conference rooms, and to the set of double doors that led into the Beaumont Theater. He had to throw his weight back to get the tall door open. The pitch-black inside was so absolute that it seemed to shine out, and he was grateful to take cover inside it.

The darkness manifested as a thick black backdrop on which the light from the bright hallway that stained his eyes swirled and drifted. His insides, that inelegantly packaged system of guts, roiled with aftershocks from Tomiina's gaze. She became a liability by simply standing there doing nothing at all. Could he afford another episode on the clock? Damian would surely fire him or humiliate him further. Movement inside of him rolled from his chest to his head, pressing him like dough against his bones. Lionel withdrew the lighter from his pocket and lit the space around him.

As he walked down the central aisle, the lighter illuminated red velvet theater seats. Their once lustrous number plates were dull and dusty. Beyond the front row, he crossed to a set of stairs and climbed on stage. Letting the lighter go out, he took center stage and made a pretentious face, stretching his arms out wide in a triumphant pose, triggering a coughing fit that echoed in the empty theater.

Flicking the lighter again, he sauntered toward the stage left wing where he found a pulley system for the curtains and a wooden ladder leading to the prop loft. After a moment of deliberation, he pocketed the lighter and slowly ascended in the dark, struggling to stay balanced. At the top, he crawled onto a plywood platform and lit the space, but there was little to see—old sheets, paint jars, wooden slats, all under a layer of dust. His knee pressed against a raised texture, something embedded in the plywood, and he brought the lighter to it. It was an arc of small indents, symmetrical with another arc beneath it. They appeared to be human teeth, inlaid into the floor neatly and purposefully in the shape of a bite. He squinted at them, his mouth hanging open wider than usual.

The hotel lobby cleared out save for a few employees behind the check-in counter and sun-tired guests at the bar. String lights wound around the coral trees outside shone through the windows. Lionel, calm after hiding in the dark for a few hours, crossed through the lobby and found Tomiina there. His knees lurched reflexively, but he pretended he didn't notice her. The muscles in his neck stiffened, and his shoulders tightened and rose as though someone dumped cold water on him.

Tomiina approached Lionel, and as the distance between them closed, his arms anxiously demanded direction. All control of his face was gone.

When he thought he morphed it into something acceptable, a silly grin appeared. As she reached him, Lionel attempted to give a casual nod of recognition, but his head jerked upward spasmodically. She opened her mouth to speak, but his phone rang. It got twisted in the fabric in his pocket, and freeing it required both of his hands. Lee Furnival was calling.

"I've got to take this," said Lionel. "Important legal business."

Tomiina nodded.

"Lee, how the heck are ya? ... Yes, this is Lionel... How would you know how I usually talk?" Lionel rolled his eyes toward Tomiina. Her smile tightened and her eyebrows went up. "The hours are really getting to me... Feels like full-time to me... I have the next few days off... Do you think I should quit? ... Can't you give me *non*-legal advice? ... Can I get a ride? ... Hello?"

Lionel pocketed his phone.

"My grandpa's lawyer. He died."

"Your grandpa's lawyer?"

"What? Oh." Lionel laughed a little too hard. "My grandpa died, and my—"

"I'm so sorry to hear."

Lionel feigned solemnity. "Oh, yes, it's been... disappointing. There's an estate sale at his house tomorrow, and I get the first look at everything before they open it up to the public."

Tomiina clutched her hands against her heart. "I've been looking for an end table. Estate sales are a gold mine for mid-century modern furniture."

"Word."

"How about I go with you?"

"That would be..." Lionel swallowed hard. "...chill."

"I would really like that." She gazed into his eyes.

Lionel checked over his shoulder, certain she had him confused with someone else, but no tall handsome man stood behind him. Surprising him further, Tomiina's hand reached toward him, and her eyes looked him up and down. The erection in his wrinkled pants could have burst through the teeth of his zipper. She tugged on his sleeve.

"Take this off right now."

"W-what?"

"Your shirt. It looks a little funky."

"I'd better not." Lionel glanced at the onlookers.

"Come on. Off."

Lionel hunched even lower than usual, lifting his shirt over his head. Tomiina waited with her hands on her hips, watching him. A tall woman and her sunburned husband openly gawked at his body, and the lady behind the check-in counter scribbled something on a pad of paper with a look of disapproval on her face. Lionel shook the sleeves off his arms, and at last he stood shirtless in the lobby, looking to Tomiina for further instructions.

She grabbed the shirt from him with two fingers and held it away from her at a distance. As her eyes flickered down to his pink, veiny belly, Lionel looked away like a dog caught peeing in the lawn.

"I'll see you tomorrow then," said Tomiina. "What time should we meet?"

"Uh... It opens at 5:30 a.m., but I'm supposed to go before it opens up." Her smile faltered. "It's down in Palos Verdes, so I guess we should leave here at... 3:45 in the morning?"

"Great. I'll go get some sleep."

Lionel stood frozen, watching her walk away. After too long, he hugged his torso and dashed out of the lobby.

Later that night, a bellboy knocked on Lionel's door. He was there to deliver a stack of stylish shirts of varying colors and patterns, all brand new.

"I think you have the wrong room."

"You are Lionel Lancet, yes?"

"Yes."

"They were sent to you by Tomiina Deatherage."

The bellboy unloaded the shirts in Lionel's arms and left.

Lionel set them on top of the dresser next to his bed and sat on the far side of the room. Lighting a joint, he eyed the shirts as if they might try to sneak up on him, which seemed more likely than the surreal truth that they were sent to him by a celebrity. Perhaps his reality was starting to align with a destiny fit for his supposed intelligence that always eluded him when he tried to invoke it, and only someone of Tomiina's status and beauty could perceive it. He didn't exhibit anything particularly attractive during their encounter, but this only bolstered his assumption that she was drawn to him because of something essential and effortless about himself.

Dirty shirts of his lay strewn across the floor, one of them torn in half. He took a long pull from the joint and set it on a coaster he was using as an ashtray, rising to try on a beige tunic from Tomiina's stack. It was from her sister Violet's fashion line, *Drab*. He admired himself in the mirror, standing taller, resembling a plump prince from a fairy tale.

After changing back into his robe and carefully hanging the shirts in his closet, he settled in a chair on his villa's back porch with one leg crossed over the other to prop up his laptop, giving an x-rated view to the fire. It occurred to him that he had scheduled a date with a movie star.

Lionel spelled Tomiina's name wrong a few times in the search bar, but he finally arrived at a video interview of her promoting a film called *Male Gayz*.

"So do you want to turn all men gay?" said the interviewer.

"That's just the kind of person I am," said Tomiina with a twinkle in her eye, pathologically charming. The interviewer snickered off camera. Tomiina relished in the attention. "I want to turn all men gay."

Among the numerous inheritances from her family, Tomiina expressed the irrational verve with which aesthetes frustrated more rigid thinkers like Lionel. She was forcefully charismatic, and she laughed too hard in self-satisfaction, which drew a silence when she stopped.

After a well-timed beat, inspired by a whim, she said, "But I think it's essential men take a look at the way they view women and realize that until they view themselves as a potential object of male sexual attention, they will never be able to relate to women."

"Incredible," said the interviewer.

Lionel rolled his eyes.

"And you see a lot of this play out with problematic men in society, some of whom go on to commit acts of violence." Tomiina spoke with exquisite command of words, but she gave the impression that she was gathering momentum to arrive at a point rather than share one she had thought of before. "Take incels. Their whole thing is that they feel fundamentally incapable of having sex with women. Maybe they're right.

Maybe they're gay, but they've been taught to be attracted to women, and they know somehow that that's impossible for them."

"I like that a lot," said the interviewer. "That is truly fascinating. And your character in the film is so dynamic."

"Thank you. Yes, I think Charlotte is a subversion of the manic pixie dream girl. But she has a lot more agency, in spite of the antagonist's attempt to take that away. So she has agency, and she doesn't, you know? It's a juxtaposition, really, but that's only apparent through a viewer assessing how their desire to know her as a type influences the effect of her character in the film."

"It's really striking. And so different from you in real life."

"It's my job as an actress to disappear so the character can come through. Like, the more you know about me in real life, the more you'll project that onto my characters. I don't think I've ever played a character that's like myself."

"Absolutely amazing," said the interviewer. Tomiina held her smile longer than Lionel was comfortable with. "So what's next?"

Tomiina shifted and looked into the space in front of her, giving the camera her all. "I just want to continue inspiring–"

Lionel grimaced and clicked back to the search results.

Another link brought him to a trashy entertainment news site that was interrupted time and again by virus alert scams and anachronistic popups, but it told him...

The advent of the superhero movie craze coincided with Eli Deatherage's advancement to senior producer at Good Tab Studios. He spearheaded Good Tab's nascent partnership with Anti-Sparrow Productions, the studio behind *The Incredulous Slag* reboot. After ten years of consistent success, they put him in charge of *Carriers of the Cosmos,* and the rest is history. His kids' kids' kids' would eat well and attend top universities. Except for Tomiina's progeny, which seemed unlikely to ever make it to term. She wanted no part in any of Eli's projects since *The Incredulous Slag,* which prompted her to tweet a 22-part screed against the film's "atrocious portrayal of women, glorification of patriarchal mores, not to mention its misuse of the word 'ironic' on several occasions..." among other complaints.

The tweets generated more buzz around the already popular film, so Eli spun it to the angry studio heads at Anti-Sparrow that it was a publicity stunt. But his daughter's tweets hurt his feelings. Only days before the tirade, he fought to get her a role as a courageous protester in the sequel, *The Incredulous Slag II: The Believening.*

She didn't go any easier on the first installment of *Carriers of the Cosmos* (for which five more installments were planned), blasting on Twitter the film's "absence of larger themes in a cosmic backdrop that simultaneously demands and denies them." Her father offered her a role even though he knew she would turn it down.

Tomiina carved out a niche for herself in independent films, low-budget, occasionally comedic dramas featuring twenty-somethings just trying to figure it out in expensive apartments in New York and LA. She would never admit that she had a type, but her roles rarely strayed from a potential love interest who inevitably refuses to derail her life for love. At the end of many of her films, she let down Tom, Dick, or Harriet with a monologue about needing to be free, or needing to put out the fires in Australia, in one case.

"Would it kill you to be in a movie where you end up in a stable relationship?" said Eli. She wouldn't hear any of it. He even offered to let her write a female-led *Carrier's of the Cosmos* spin-off to rid the franchise of the "male gaze," a term she taught him during production of her film of the same name. As always, she declined.

Her breakout role was Astrid Cabral, the owner of a bowling alley in a neighborhood that's slowly being taken over by entitled yuppies. One such yuppie could bowl well over 220. His urban garb and filterless cigarettes trick Astrid into believing he was from the neighborhood, and the two fall in love. But when the critics of gentrification take to the streets, Astrid finds herself on the other side of the protest line as Drew. In an instant, she realizes his clothes were made to look dingy and that she had never seen him actually smoke a cigarette.

The remainder of the film amounted to a screed about male entitlement, the plight of the working class, and a last-minute conflict where the yuppy tries to buy her bowling alley with his parents' money, which is settled by a bowl-off that Astrid wins by rolling a 7-10 split, angering the yuppy so much that he falls to the ground, knocking over a rack of bowling balls, one of which falls on his bowling hand, breaking all the bones in his fingers. The final scene is Astrid talking to her girlfriends who got almost no screen time and whose names are shoehorned in to squeak out a marginal passing grade on the Bechdel test, only to fail it moments later by her mentioning that the preceding romantic entanglement depicted as the dominant narrative action in the film is not even close to the biggest thing going on in her life, considering her daily struggle against The Man. The whole thing was supposed to be a departure from romantic movies: no one gets the girl, the girl gets herself, and the yuppy moves back to the suburbs to nurse his hand back to health.

Gentrify My Heart didn't last in theaters, and it was ridiculed in the festival circuit, but streaming services picked it up and viewership was good enough to get her a five-film deal.

Her first film for streaming services got lukewarm reviews in spite of the melodramatic writing and her Oscar-bait performance as a vlogger who fights for respect online after an HIV diagnosis. No one had the heart to critique *Positive Representation.*

Her performance as a sex worker with disabilities in *Weakest Kink* was critically panned.

The internet loved her as a local art dealer who struggles to live green in a severe drought in *Kitsch out of Water*, but by the time she aimed to subvert the woman in peril as a perfectly capable woman trapped in a furniture store in *Night in Shining Armoire,* critics settled on her status as an indulgent try-hard who wouldn't be surprising anyone anytime soon.

Tomiina's socially conscious films received praise on Twitter, but more than a few death threats came her way, such as "I want to set Tomena Dethrage on fire" and "I want to murder that whore" and "Tomiina Deatherage deserves to be raped and murdered" and "Can someone shoot this bitch already?" Plenty of her fans waged tweet-wars on her behalf, but not everyone was moved by the supposed plight of a celebrity. Conservative accounts were quick to point out the threats and murder plots were hollow.

However, progressive voices did not universally accept her. One blogger wrote: "It's difficult to suspend my disbelief that someone who's practically a Disney is fighting against the man." Breaking her rule of not engaging with critics, she responded that she had publicly criticized her father's films and that she had not received a penny of their profits, but she left the exchange that ensued when she caught sight of a tweet from an uninvolved party that said, "It's as though Tomiina Deatherage was coached to have flaws to humanize her."

There were no flaws that Lionel could see. He searched for nude pictures of her, but finding none, decided that a photo of her in a low-cut top would suffice. He began to masturbate. What about him drew her in? Nothing he did should have earned him that encounter, but it happened and there was a roomful of witnesses. And crazier still, she was choosing to spend time with him again on purpose.

After he finished, it dawned on him that he could never be with her. He must have gotten caught up in the celebrity hype. She was a movie star, and she had charmed him. She probably did that to everybody. The cleft of one of his man-boobs emerged into the cold air, and he adjusted the hem of his robe to hide it.

Lionel navigated to YouTube to watch atheists deliver cutting retorts to believers. Recently, he was on a kick of watching Sam Harris, the neuroscientist/public intellectual whose cold monotone and advocacy for the benefits of secular meditation evoked a sense of fairness that Lionel saw as a concession to critics of Hitchens's and Dawkins's often insulting style. His interest in Harris indicated his own intellectual maturation to himself. But another video caught his eye.

Although Lionel was no believer in fate—that higher order to the universe that might steer him one way or another—he developed a cache of browsing data that fed YouTube's algorithm which orchestrated an inevitability to his recommended videos. For sacred reasons known only to coders in Silicon Valley, Lionel's demographics plus his interest in atheism made him all but destined to click a video titled "Liberal Crybabies DESTROYED with Undeniable Truth."

A man in a flamboyant scarf wrapped around him and dyed blonde hair sat in an armchair with his legs crossed. He was on a stage in a college auditorium, smug and bored like Lou Reed behind sunglasses. A student in a navy blazer talked into a mic at a podium.

"We are thankful that, in spite of a number of students on campus attempting to stop us, we were able to get one of the most daring voices in contemporary thought." The crowd applauded, but jeering sounded in the background, which the seated man in shades met with a mocking frown, pretending to rub tears out of his eyes. "I'm sure most of you are familiar with his work, so I'll wrap it up and let him speak for himself."

"Please do, love," said the stylish man.

The crowd laughed in approval.

"Without further ado, Milo Yiannopoulos!"

Milo stood and reveled in the applause. When it died down, he encouraged it to continue, and it temporarily returned before he finally waved it off.

"Hello, everyone. I'm so thrilled that you invited a racist, bigot, homophobe to come and corrupt you all." Laughter and cheering from the crowd. "They call me a white supremacist, even though I have a black husband. They call me an idiot, but they won't even debate me. They're offended by my words, and I have a message for them: *good*. If you're offended by what I have to say, good. I am a provocateur, and I know I will scare people away with my ideas, but those who actually listen to what I have to say will realize that what I'm saying is true."

Like most Americans, Lionel conferred intellectual authority on anyone with a British accent. The mixture of condescension and articulation intimidated him into passivity that made people on his side of the pond actually listen, an intellectual Stockholm syndrome in relation to the former colonial overlords which would never be offered to a fellow national.

Milo was the heir to the combative style of Dawkins and Hitchens, but he updated it with theatricality and bitchy panache. There was something brave and defiant about his willingness to speak out against his opponents. While Lionel's favorite atheists served devastating comebacks, Milo did so while standing up to a horde of college students rushing his stage, determined to shout him down and shut him up. In doing so, they only proved Milo's point: that contemporary society was hostile to white men and the conservative point of view.

This was hardly a new idea. Conservatives had been complaining for decades about the liberal dominance of universities and the media. The thrust of Milo's message might as well have been lifted from the 1971 Powell Memorandum, which laid the foundation for the conservative movement and a slew of right-wing think tanks that came after. In his memo titled "Attack on American Free Enterprise System," attorney Lewis F. Powell Jr., who was then only months away from accepting a Supreme Court nomination under Nixon, wrote a plan for corporate interests to take back America and defend it against "broad attack." While subversive factions and revolutionaries were mentioned, the "Sources of the Attack" were identified as "the college campus, the pulpit, the media, the intellectual and literary journals, the arts and sciences..."

This network, spanning a wide range of industries and institutions, was dubbed The Cathedral as late as 2008 by neo-reactionary blogger Curtis Yarvin, known better by his pen name Mencius Moldbug, and he got a lot of mileage out of the religious backdrop of this comparison. Citing historian Carlton Hayes's 1924 addendum to his 1916 book *History of Modern Europe* wherein Hayes wrote of the unification among various "Progressive" Protestant sects to which unwilling "Fundamentalists" reacted and dug in their heels and refused to conform lest they forgo the dogma of their particular denominations, Moldbug noted the similarity between this Protestant Progressive vs. Fundamentalist conflict and America's contemporary blue-state vs. red-state conflict. Just as Hayes treated the growing unification among sects as the mainstream and the Fundamentalists as aberrant stragglers behind the progression of history, so too, Moldbug argued, do cultural and political progressives of modern-day regard themselves as having arrived at the truth while their conservative opponents labor under the delusion of an outdated religious sect that couldn't keep up with the times.

Moldbug demonstrated that this "truth" espoused by progressives was simply a tradition, not unlike a religious sect, whose ubiquity and dominance was simply a matter of historical tendency, and that they hadn't arrived at any certain declaration of validity in spite of their near total reign. As an atheist himself, he certainly didn't advocate for theism or bemoan the removal of god from schools, but rather, Moldbug invited readers of his blog *Unqualified Reservations* to see the religious nature of progressive institutions: "Harvard and Stanford and Yale are fundamentalist seminaries. It may not be official, but there is no doubt about it at all. They emit Jesus-freak codewords, secret Mormon handshakes, and miscellaneous Bible baloney the way a baby emits fermented milk... If you find the exercise unpalatable, dear open-minded progressive, just snap the Fundamentalens [*sic*] back on and imagine you're trying to free your government from the icy inexorable grip of Jesus."

Heretofore, these complaints had come from balding corporate suits with bad skin and bloggers like Moldbug, who was a computer programmer and looked like one. But Milo Yiannopoulos wore leopard print suit jackets and designer shades, which often stayed on during his appearances. He was gay and catty, qualities that even young men on the right-wing knew conferred authority on all things vogue. And with the funds from billionaire Robert Mercer and Glittering Steel LLC, chaired by conservative political strategist Steve Bannon, Milo made these decades-old ideas seem edgy, subversive, and new.

But Lionel only saw unruly students storming the stage, shouting and blowing whistles, trying to shut down a perfectly rational speaker. Opponents of Dawkins and Hitchens attempted to engage with their ideas at least. They would trade arguments, and the truth would win out. That's how it was supposed to work in a civilized society. But Milo's opponents threatened to destroy the spirit of rational debate, a spirit that animated Western civilization, all in the name of their religious fundamentalism, invading the space of this lone warrior and trouncing his right to free speech. It was in this way that Milo's corporate-sponsored point of view seemed like a daring counterstrike against a powerful adversary.

"And they'll call me a racist because that's what they call anyone who disagrees with them," said Milo, obscured behind the group of students on his stage. "But nothing in my message is even about race. It's about the West. And Western values have never faced a greater threat than they do today–"

Someone cut Milo's mic, and boos from the crowd joined the cacophony of the protestors on stage. Lionel sat up in his chair, his heart rate elevating with the commotion as though he were in the auditorium. The students' arrogance, their sheer self-importance to cast themselves as heroes and arbitrarily choose a villain to fight, resonated as base disgust in him more than registering as opposition to his vague intellectual foundation. His favorite atheists cited the West's rich intellectual history that spanned thousands of years, but there before his eyes, a group of fanatics caught up in a religious fervor were not trying to disprove it. They were trying to destroy it, threatening to plunge the world not just into delusion but into aimless, violent chaos. Lionel leaned closer to the screen.

Chapter 9

A company called Get the Worm organized the estate sale at Art Lancet's house, and eager early birds posted up at four o'clock in the morning to have first pick of his belongings. The line forming outside his house was the only disruption to the suburban stillness in the dark of the early morning, but there was a tense silence among the shoppers waiting. Competition for rarities rivaled Black Friday's capacity to bring out the worst in its customers, and everyone who knew what was good for them came prepared to engage in a tug of war or even a fight. It was Constance, out of the goodness of her heart, who suggested that Lionel do a walk-through before the sale opened to pick out items that might remind him of his grandfather. But Lee Furnival made it clear on the phone that Lionel was not entitled to any of the money liquidated from the sale.

The coast got the coldest just before sunrise, and Tomiina and Lionel shivered as they exited his Lexus. The breeze swam right inside the broad neckline of Lionel's new tunic. Every eye in line followed them as they ambled to the front door, Tomiina with her head down, and a Get the Worm employee verified Lionel's identity and let them in, which was met with jeering and cries of foul play.

A cash register was set up in the living room, just outside the entryway, and knickknacks sat in rows in clear plastic display cases on tables against the walls. The door to the home office on the other side of the entryway stood open, and the room was gutted save for a card table with Art's stone lingam, plaques, and marble ashtray, which all sported price tags.

Pressing farther inside, Lionel and Tomiina entered the master bedroom. Get the Worm had Art's dressers, loungers, and coffee tables lined up like inventory at a warehouse, and his mattress and bed frame were turned on their sides and leaning against the wall. In the kitchen, there was a hope chest with nothing in it, and Art's clothes and linens deemed suitable for sale lay folded on a circular, glass-top table for which the asking price stood at $6,500.

Constance smoked a cigarette on the back patio where flowerpots stood in rows with a strip of tape connecting them on which someone wrote in sharpie "Not for Sale." Lionel exited the kitchen, careful not to make a sound.

In the living room, Art's belongings were laid out on tables—surf wax in shoe boxes, a complete catalog of Playboy magazines from March 1973 to 2001, cigar cutters, one of which was designed to look like a woman's crotch where the cigar was inserted, a heavily worn copy of the Tibetan Book of the Dead, burned down candles in wax flecked candelabras with serpentine ironwork, an ornate trunk-handled elephant goad, and Art's surfboard, leaning in the corner.

For the first time since Lionel could remember, he felt pressure to see the objects in front of him as representative of something more than their mass. His grandfather's belongings should have exhibited a ghostly radiance now that he was gone or transience lurking within them as the house was about to be ravaged by strangers. He searched inside himself for sentimentality, however dim, for the assortment before him, willing tears to come as if he were relenting to his grandfather's absence, but when his eyes watered it was only from the dust in the air.

"You are definitely taking this," said Tomiina, entering from the kitchen and beelining to the elephant goad.

"What is it?"

"An Ankusha. It's one of the Eight Auspicious Signs of the Ashtamangala. I wonder if he has any more."

"The eight what of what now?"

"The Eight Auspicious Signs of the Ashtamangala."

Lionel nodded as though he were well-versed in all eight, but he went through the labor of asking, "Remind me, what's the Ashton...?"

"They're symbols used in Hinduism and Buddhism."

"That's really cool." Lionel's eyes were dead.

"Isn't it?" Tomiina brought her face close to his.

The emotional vacancy in him graciously accepted her gaze, and his mouth opened slightly. His focus softened, and the fluttering in his stomach had him grasping the edge of the display table so he wouldn't fall over. Mounting energy inside of him demanded release, and he found it in a sneeze that sprayed like a shotgun in her face.

They were both mortified. Tomiina lunged at him with the elephant goad, stopping short of stabbing Lionel in the chest.

"I am so sorry." Lionel searched his surroundings for anything to alleviate the situation, and his eyes landed on the Play Boys. He stared at them, pretending to give her a dignified moment free of his attention. With a moist towelette from her purse, she wiped her face many times over while inspecting herself in a compact mirror. After composing herself, she broke the silence that settled, smiling.

"That was truly horrific."

"I don't know where that came from," said Lionel. "It happened so fast."

"Didn't you ever learn to cover your mouth?"

"I don't usually sneeze around other people." Tomiina accepted this as the end of it but got confused considering what he said. "Don't you want the... thing?" said Lionel, pointing to the elephant goad.

"Nah, I've got a few at home."

Footsteps sounded in the hallway leading to the foyer, and Lionel's stomach sank with the expectation that emotional demands were headed his way. Constance and he met during a brief Christmas dinner years ago over which Art and Francis maintained single-minded focus on the papers they passed between them, and he answered her polite questions without bothering to conceal how burdensome he found the interaction. There was levity to her as she appeared in the living room, even with tears in her dark eyes. She wore all black, and her hand massaged her jaw.

"Lionel." Constance crossed the room to embrace him, which he met stiffly. "You must be devastated."

"Yes. Very sad."

Tomiina hugged Constance.

"Is this your girlfriend?"

Lionel stood taller, emboldened by the implication. Constance seeing him out with Tomiina brought their as yet undefined relationship down to earth from the lofty heights of his imagination, where it had been hard to believe. It was the observer effect, carving out a Lionel-shaped hole in the ether for him to abide in. He began to regard his isolation and obscurity as a training ground, a series of trials to prepare him for his new essence that would pervade his interior, and the world was starting to take notice.

"We haven't labeled it," said Tomiina.

"Cherish her, Lionel," said Constance. "Cultivate your love, and she will serve you and respect your leadership." Tomiina's eye twitched. "You probably want to be alone, but I had to see you. How have you been handling everything?"

"I'm getting by. But the hours are getting to me."

"You're working? Full time?"

"No."

Constance smiled. "You're so much like him." She reached her hand out to touch his cheek, and he leaned away to avoid it. The hand went back to comforting her jaw. "You have his face."

"Must be genetic." He looked to Tomiina, who avoided his eyes.

"I will leave you to mourn in peace, but I need to talk to you privately."

"Take all the time you need," said Tomiina, with a sympathetic touch on Constance's shoulder, and she crossed to the home office and shut the door behind her. Constance's eyes were locked on Lionel's, and they filled with more tears.

"I never wanted to destroy Art's marriage."

"Oh did you guys—"

"I was responsible for your grandmother leaving him."

In the late 80s, a vague plan to be an actress brought Constance from France to Los Angeles, and a chance encounter with Art at a bar shifted her career path toward housekeeping and Art toward infidelity. But in spite of her moving in and replacing Art's wife, she kept to her duties, sweeping, polishing, cooking, cleaning, dusting, and laughing on cue when Art cracked a joke. He told Constance that she held him together after the years tried to break him into pieces. The fellow members of the Fiduciary Royalties Association for United Donors noticed him glowing each time she entered the room to serve them. She never went on a single audition.

"Word."

"We loved. Passionately."

"I see."

"In the kitchen, the hallway, on that chair."

Lionel was touching a recliner, and he inspected his hand for residue, tight-lipped. He wiped his palm on his pant leg, just in case.

A wave of sadness descended on Constance, and Lionel absorbed it as well, but he drew away from her. Her pain seemed to cross the space between them as though she transmitted it psychically. Lionel swallowed the feeling. Tomiina could come back at any moment, and he intended that she find him dry-eyed.

"There's something else."

"Oh?"

"He blamed me."

"For his divorce?"

"For the lawsuits."

"For the lawsuits? Why?"

"He thought I was the reason that his foundation was getting into legal trouble. I knew nothing about his business. I wouldn't even know what to tell anyone. But he was convinced that I reported him. I was worried for him, and I can be weepy and afraid, but he took that for guilt and disloyalty. That's what he said, 'There's more to your story, Constance. You're hiding something, Constance.'"

"Why did he think that? What did he think you were hiding?"

"I'm really sorry, Lionel. I wish I could tell you more. But I know nothing. I don't think he even knew what he thought I did. He was very paranoid before he died. He said, 'Only someone this close to me could have betrayed me,' and 'You ruined the integrity of my foundation.' He wouldn't look at me. When I tried to talk to him, he said, 'Yes, Constance. Good, Constance.' But his face is blank, and he's far away in some other place in his head.

"I would never betray him. He didn't believe me." She started sobbing, and she returned her hand to her jaw. "Right up to the end. He pointed at me like this." She pointed her finger. "And his face was like this." She narrowed her eyes, making a mean face, which relented to more tears. "And he said nothing, but there was so much anger. He was sure it was me. They wouldn't even let me go to his funeral."

The inclination to comfort her occurred to him, and he brought his hand to her shoulder, but worry for himself throttled inside of him at the reminder that the lawsuits were still on.

"Do you believe me, Lionel?"

"I believe you."

"I wouldn't even know how to tell the FBI."

"The FBI?"

"It's really bad, Lionel."

"But I thought—This is California. Everyone's in a lawsuit."

"Not like this one, I'm afraid."

Lionel swallowed. Those three letters inspired his insides to roil and drift about, and a dewy layer of sweat started on his palms. He thrust his tongue against his soft palate, urging a glob of mucus resting in his postnasal cavity to drip down, but it hung on.

Constance hugged him.

"I miss him too. I was there. My hands were on his chest. I felt him slip away. It was like my whole life led to that moment... to deliver him safely to the afterlife."

She released the hug and brought her face close to his. Lionel nodded, as speaking was out of the question. Everything in his periphery pulsated toward him as if the room were trying to choke him, and stars darted in tight coils around Constance's face.

"If you ever need anything, I'm here for you, Lionel. I can guide you."

As Constance left the living room, Lionel could think only to put his hands on his hips, pretending that pressure in his ears wasn't radiating in small pulses across his brain and recalibrating his sense of balance.

The moment she was gone, he sprang into action, trying to tear his tunic in half, but in a brief moment of lucidity, he took it off carefully and folded it, gasping for air. The horizon tilted, and he followed it, falling against the wall. He walked his hands down and landed in a crouch to panic safely on the floor. The assemblage of his grandfather's belongings throbbed as a single mass and vanished beneath a shifting surface of color, a semiotic field emitted from heirlooms and knickknacks alike which signified a broad range of meanings that raced through his head too quickly for him to interpret. His interior began to float beyond his ribs, and he had to lurch and grab at it to keep it contained.

In the home office, a small sliver of light from the window reflected off something in the corner toward Tomiina. She crouched for a better look and traced the outline of the compartment with her finger. It drew her in as though sounding a call only to those attuned to its quiet, mystical frequency. The opening revealed the serpent-handled dagger, and she took it into her hands, red and white shimmering from the inlaid jewels.

Hubbub from the outside alerted Lionel that the masses were about to enter. His episode subsided, and he managed to climb back into his tunic. An employee from Get the Worm yelled, "You can shove each other, but if you touch any of the employees we'll ask you to—*ahh!*" Lionel rose to his feet as shoppers pressed their faces against the window to get a look at the loot.

Feeling pressured to leave with something, Lionel fit as many Playboys as he could into a bag. They were modest compared to the orgies his internet browser could summon with a few keystrokes, but he reasoned they were collector's items. On the mantle above the fireplace, there was a cigar box with a headdress-clad Native American on the lid and tucked it under his arm as he made for the door.

Chapter 10

As if the antiques and heirlooms at the estate sale were not enough, Tomiina signed them up for another treasure hunt at Abalone Cove Shoreline Park, just a short drive from Art's house. The high tide washed colorful creatures and beautiful shells into the crater-like tide pools at the base of the cliffs, and at low tide, they were trapped and easily viewable as a naturally assembled aquatic menagerie.

The news about the FBI soured Lionel's stomach, and he didn't realize that he was hungry until he stopped to catch his breath on the footpath that led from the parking lot, through cliffs, to the beach and tide pools below. Ignoring his misery, Tomiina primed him for the exotic creatures they were about to see—sea hares that looked gross but smelled fresh and piny, bright colorful slugs like real-life Pokémon, purple urchins wedged in almost every crevice, anemones and their tentacles that resembled faded flower petals. Slick black crabs were known to crawl around everywhere, and they might even see sea lions, which are different from seals. She interrupted her spiel on the Pacific gray whale's migration pattern to say, as a matter of grave importance, "If you see starfish, you need to tell me. Right away."

Lionel glared back at her.

Tomiina decided that he was done resting and skipped away. The rest of his descent became pained clomping, each step a short fall from which he caught himself with a straight leg, threatening to ruin his knees. A cactus leaned into the path, and he gave it a wide berth. When the hedges cleared, he saw Tomiina stepping deftly across the rounded rocks on the beach, and she broke into a sprint upon reaching the sand.

Seismic motion frequently vibrated out of the fault line running along the coast, shifting the land and splitting deep crevices close to where the footpath let out to the beach. Lionel trudged over the rocks and sand and past a sign at the edge of the tide pools that warned of falling rocks.

Giant, yellow-brown stone slabs outcropped from the sand like rows of elephant teeth. They were embedded with ancient lines of sediment, uneven steps leading to the tide pools. Tomiina hopped from rock to rock, snapping pictures on her phone. Behind her, turquoise water ate a cave into the base of the cliffs, and kelp waved in and out with it like streamers in the wind. Someone built a clubhouse out of stone and sand at the mouth of the cave, complete with tiki torches and a roof made of dried palm fronds.

There was a clear view out to Catalina Island. A lone surfer lay belly down on their board past the rocks, paddling lazily, bobbing in the waves.

"This is an anemone. Watch this." Tomiina dipped her finger in the anemone's center, and it closed its tentacles softly. "Sensual." She grabbed Lionel's hand to steer it toward the opening, but he pulled away. "It's harmless."

"Aren't there ocean diseases?"

She guided his hand into the water, and as the anemone closed around his finger, he grimaced, violated by its surprisingly rubbery texture.

"Starfish!" Bending over with her butt in his face, she hugged her hands to her heart, swooning.

As she admired the orange starfish, Lionel admired her butt. It put him in a trance, and in spite of his fear of its power over him, he could not look away nor express anything but awe. When she turned back to him, he looked to the ground and then the sky.

"Are you okay?"

"Yeah. I'm good. Constance said the FBI might be after me."

She touched her hand to his and gave him a close-up-worthy sympathetic beat. "That must be really hard."

"It's something about these lawsuits... I don't really get it. It seems like it's all about my grandpa, so I'll probably be fine."

"Unless it's guilt by association."

"But what's he guilty of? He was just an old rich guy. That doesn't really hurt anybody."

"Wealth can have a lot of consequences for the underprivileged."

"Yeah, but he's dead. I think this whole thing is going to blow over."

Tomiina studied him for a moment, pregnant with deliberation. It took all of his courage to look back at her when her face expressed anything other than approval. Lapping waves filled the silence, reduced from their crashing at the edge of the craters, washing toward the puddles where they stood.

"We explored the legal but morally fraught actions of the rich in *Gentrify My Heart*," said Tomiina. "It's streaming on like every platform."

"I don't really watch movies."

"*I don't really watch movies,*" said Tomiina, mocking him.

Lionel was taken aback. He felt some unknown failure of his knocked Tomiina out of alignment with the version of her he earned through his natural intelligence and essence, which manifested as her unconditional approval thus far. In an instant, his conception of her ascended out of reach, and grasping at it would only spill him out of any semblance of security that contained him.

"Actually, that's refreshing," she said. "You know, you're not like anyone I've ever met. I like that you don't try too hard."

"At what?" Lionel braced himself for more emotional whiplash.

"Anything, really. Everyone I know is always striving and climbing. I like that you don't do that."

Lionel shrugged and looked away. Just like that, he nestled back into the embrace of his self-image as someone who was fundamentally valid, as though her affection traced a stencil around him and provided a warm enclosure.

Chancing a look back, he found that Tomiina faced him still, reserving the right to look him up and down without any regard that he noticed her assessing him. The demands of the day, all the chemicals that fired through him in flashes of panic and ticklish bursts of smitten admiration brought raw fatigue to the core of his head. It would take a joint and a nap to recharge his capacity to look back at her without squirming. Even the sun, fixed at an angle to shine right in his eyes no matter where he stood, conspired to eat away at his composure.

Tomiina shrieked excitedly, and the sound ground him down further in an oppressive wave. He apprehended her passions with reluctant awe. They seemed so arbitrary to him, but she treated all her whims as the most obvious course of action, as real and concrete as the craggy rocks she bounded over, moving toward something he couldn't see. At the edge of the tide, she grabbed a glimmering stone that washed up on shore and held it proudly above her head.

"Do you know how rare these are?"

Lionel looked at the mass of water-smoothed rocks along the beach, the chipped fragments beside him from the cliffs above, the crags jutting out around the cave, and the brick red and blue-gray stones crowded in the tide pools.

"Not that rare," said Lionel, walking toward the sand. There was a long, hilly walk ahead of him, and he started it with his head down.

"This is a moonstone. They used to be all over Redondo, but the locals overharvested them. They aren't supposed to make it this far south."

"Fascinating."

"They're good luck. This could be the last one left." She trotted over to him, holding the moonstone out in front of her. "I want you to have it."

"I don't believe in luck."

"It works whether you believe in it or not." She offered it to him with a salesman's panache. He kept on moping, trudging toward the footpath.

Tomiina scowled at his intransigence and crouched down to draw in the sand. Lionel feigned disinterest, but he stopped to watch her scraping and etching with the moonstone. What started as a date or at least a pleasant day out was no longer anything he could identify, but there was no fight left in him. Without objecting, his eyes wandered to her drawing, and it transfixed him instantly as though its shape bypassed his rational mind to communicate with his subconscious. A strong wind whipped around him, lifting loose sand into a shapeless spray. The tide was rising.

The lone surfer observed them from afar.

Before becoming an attorney, Melanie Bobbers rolled with an all-female surf crew called The Surf Skanks, whose constituents were fed up with the male-dominated, territorial surf culture in Southern California that made it almost impossible to catch a wave without getting burned. The Surf Skanks developed a reputation for putting men to shame from Manhattan Beach to Malibu with a supportive, communitarian ethic, banishing anyone who tried to claim ownership of waves that should be free to everyone.

Men threw unimaginative taunts, demanding sandwiches and sexual favors, but everybody got quiet when the Surf Skanks shredded with undeniable prowess. They actually brought sandwiches on occasion and ate furtively because of the implication, but their eventual switch to lettuce wraps circumvented the issue altogether. A critic of Melanie's online pointed out that she was technically a former member of The SS, apparent evidence of her feminazi agenda, but this was widely disregarded even among her fiercest opponents and conspiracy theorists.

Before long, it became clear to her that the male aggression dominating the surf scene went way beyond the coastline. Synchronicities dogged her—men cutting in the checkout line, men running into her on the sidewalk rather than letting her pass, men spreading their legs wide when sitting so she had to make herself small—and she predicted, moments before each encounter, that whatever space she tried to share with everyone would be claimed and defended by an entitled man.

Melanie second-guessed that she was paranoid. It wasn't impossible that she projected and created the trend by focusing on it. Certainly not every man exhibited such selfishness and disrespect. She had male friends and colleagues, and it was a man who saved her when she was trapped in a room by a group of men at a college party.

But she couldn't ignore the truth any longer. Domineering men pervaded almost every aspect of her life, and she stopped questioning why everyone regarded their bad behavior with such a permissive attitude. She decided to do something about it. Surfing became more casual to her as she started shredding men in a legal sense. But taking her board out today was anything but casual.

After extensive research, she discovered that Eli Deatherage and Art Lancet shared business interests in addition to the Hotel Bellehaven. The collage on her wall in her Highland Park office mapped the various shell companies, subsidiaries, faux-charities, and tax shelters between them as well as a trail of money that found its way to conservative think tanks. It was shaping up to be a full-blown conspiracy. Just what they conspired to do was yet to be determined, but it iterated the familiar pattern of men taking more than their share and getting away with it.

Melanie paddled to the shore to see the symbol Tomiina drew, but it was gone, washed away by the tide. She pushed back out into the water to catch a few more waves before calling it a day.

The orange of a Garibaldi fish caught her eye, and she trained her water-proof camera on it until it disappeared under some rocks. An approaching wave pointed a surfer on a trajectory aimed right at her, and she raised her hand to alert him, but the fury in his bloodshot eyes indicated that he intended to crash into her. She dove into the water at the last second.

The man was one of the Lunada Bay Boys, a gang of territorial surfers notorious for terrorizing Lunada Bay, an ideal surf spot a little to the north of Abalone Cove. They were known to vandalize cars, break surfboards, punch ribs, and throw rocks at anyone who "trespassed." Police dismissed complaints against them due to their long history in the community, some of the boys in blue being former members of the gang themselves. It was the Lunada Bay Boys who built the stone clubhouse at the mouth of the cave there in Abalone Cove, an illegal structure to which authorities turned a blind eye.

When Melanie surfaced, the Bay Boy called to her in a California whine, "You can't surf here." The Bay Boy pointed to their clubhouse by the cave.

Melanie spat out saltwater. "Bullshit. The California Coastal Act prevents private ownership on the beach."

"You've got to go. This is ours."

Two more gray-haired surfers paddled up and joined their friend.

"I thought you assholes stayed up in Lunada Bay?"

"The Coast Guard knocked down our clubhouse up there. We're the Abalone Cove Bros now."

"No, we're the Abalone Jabronis."

"We're still working on the name actually."

"So you're taking over a beach at a state park?"

"We don't recognize your laws, man."

"I'm not a man."

They laughed.

"We'll burn you at every wave."

Melanie smirked, certain that she could shred the shit out of all three of them without getting out of breath. Without warning, she paddled toward an approaching wave, and the Lunada Bay Boys went after her. The first Bay Boy was getting close, but she stood and rode the curve of the wave in front of him. He ducked down trying to close the gap, but her wake sprayed up at him and he collapsed backward off of his board.

Melanie carved forward and allowed herself a backward glance. The other two Bay Boys raced toward her, but they were so frantic in their chase that they crashed into each other, their skulls colliding, knocking both of them out cold in the water.

The waves delivered her to the edge of the tide pools, and she hoisted herself up to the entrance of their clubhouse. As she lifted her board out of the water, the Bay Boy who remained conscious paddled toward his board to keep up the chase. She couldn't help but antagonize him further by entering their clubhouse. The inside, she was surprised to find, turned out to be a vestibule that led to a hallway-like cave reaching into the cliffside, lit with an orange, halogen bulb in a spherical streetlight. She glanced behind her before advancing deeper inside, and more streetlights lit the path.

Melanie froze after rounding a corner, hearing the steps of the Bay Boy echo behind her. Perhaps she got too cocky. But maybe the path let out somewhere. She continued forward, the tunnel leading her into a big circular room with a lit torch on the wall, a few ropes on the ground, and a small chimney hole at the top. The Bay Boy's tramping in the cave came closer, and Melanie paced, searching for an escape that didn't seem to be there.

As she braced herself for a fight, it occurred to her to wield the torch. She hid next to the entrance, ready to bring a fiery crash upon him, but when he arrived, he stopped short, and her downward swing was a complete whiff. The torch crashed against the ground, the flame exploding with dancing embers, and the room went dark.

The Bay Boy laughed. "We usually have to drag people back here. Thanks for saving me the trouble."

Melanie heard his footsteps cross the room and stop.

His body collided against hers, and she scratched at his face and his eyes, thick pulp accumulating under her nails. The Bay Boy rolled off of her howling. He punched her hard in the stomach, knocking the wind out of her, and climbed on her, kneeling on her arms. There, he began to tie rope around her wrists, and once he finished, he bound her feet as she thrashed and screamed futilely.

Cold metal entered her mouth, the business end of pliers searching for a tooth. Finding one, he removed her left canine with a swift yank, and searing pain spiraled across her entire face. She shrieked, choking on a warm mouthful of blood.

"You are hereby committed to the earth: the churned and settled remains of all biological material, to nourish our food, to nourish our bodies, so that we may die one day and nurture the select few of our offspring chosen to carry on our story, our sacrificial burden to balance the cycle of life and death, on behalf of the Fiduciary Royalties Association for United Donors."

The look of horror that cracked across her face at the mention of the name of her current legal target's foundation could have made her go viral if it were not pitch black inside the cave. It released pressure in her skull, like a clenched muscle that didn't know it was tense until it relaxed.

She was not operating at peak performance after hearing her death sentence and fighting for a pardon, and being bound by rope wasn't helping matters either. Worse still, her camera was unable to capture anything since the torch went out. The most pivotal video in her social media career: audio-only.

The Bay Boy straddled her, preparing an execution in gruesome fashion hidden by the darkness, but she straightened her back against the ground and thrashed her bound legs upward, and these were experienced surfer legs, connecting powerfully with his groin. He let out a great, "*Oooo*," and crumpled to the ground.

She wriggled out of the hand ties and started to work on the ropes around her ankles. He tackled her again, and her head clunked on the floor, inspiring a breaking point that granted her the strength to push the Bay Boy off of her and begin slugging the ever-loving shit out of his face with a clenched fist, paying no mind that her feet were still bound. Once she was certain he was incapacitated, she edged over to the wall to collect herself, tonguing the soft hole in her gums that gushed with blood.

Chapter 11

Lionel kept his hand in his pocket, clutching the moonstone. The symbol he saw Tomiina draw with it in the sand meant nothing to his conscious mind, but it resonated with something deeper inside of him, that fearful something that occasionally demanded escape from the confines of his body. It reached warmth and airiness, at least until his high wore off from a small joint he smoked that morning. He willed himself to align with that weightless ether, but his insides soured again, lightyears from whatever Tomiina's symbol seemed to promise. He thumbed the moonstone greedily to no otherworldly effect. Unless there was an aura radiating out of it, its significance would remain as nothing more than its immediate form—a pretty rock.

The overcast sky lit the grounds of the Hotel Bellehaven and had everyone squinting against the dim fluorescent white. The Republican National Convention ended, and most of the rooms and rental villas emptied out. Lionel waited in the lobby like a good little boy for Damian who returned from his vacation with a plump, childish face. His features were large and colorful like a painted doll's. Above his definitively rosy cheeks, his over-dazzling eyes gleamed, but his left eyelid skewed outward, so it looked like his eyes were pointed in two different directions. Lionel smiled to conceal his curiosity at Damian's new face.

"Where did you take those boxes?"

After a long, frozen moment scrambling for something to say, Lionel had to step back to keep from tipping over.

"To the address."

"What address?"

"Tony Motion's."

"Who the fuck is Tony Motion?"

"... at the house in Holmby Hills."

"Where are they!"

Guests in the lobby looked toward them.

"At Tony's."

Lionel was sure that Damian's face would have matched his contemptuous rage if he could have gotten it to move.

"I heard you took off your shirt in the lobby again."

"Huh? Oh yeah."

"Why?"

Lionel shrugged, moping. Damian lowered his voice so only Lionel could hear. "Go get my boxes right now, or I'll tear your teeth out."

Lionel's insides went cold. The onlookers returned to their idly waiting for their rooms, for their kids who were changing into swimsuits, for the bar to open. Anyone present might have saved Lionel, but the liminal air of the lobby focused their minds elsewhere. Even those who sat did so in a state of purgatory.

Damian grabbed Lionel's hand and walked him to the check-in counter.

"Pen," he demanded of the lobby in general. A vested woman whose name tag read Carla handed Damian a pen that was well within his reach. He proceeded to write 446 Hillcrest Drive on Lionel's palm. Lionel winced, submitting as the pen gouged his skin. Indifferent faces in the lobby averted their eyes toward magazines, the ceiling, and their watches. When Damian finished writing, Lionel studied his hand so no one would see the tears in his eyes. He broke away to cross the short distance to the front entrance, where he swallowed the raw hurt down into his gut and continued to the parking lot, blank.

When Lionel returned to Tony's, Marcus, wearing a black tracksuit today, brought him to a greenhouse full of marijuana plants in the backyard. Humidity hung in the air, and mist sprayed from a system of thin pipes that lined the ceiling and softened the beams from grow lights above the rows of plants. A small cloud of smoke rose from a row in the back, and Lionel saw the top of Tony's head beneath it. He crossed toward him.

Tony had a joint between his lips, and he spread his arms in greeting when he saw Lionel. The grow light above him flickered a bit, and Tony shook its enclosure until it stayed on. The fragrant skunk smell of marijuana wafted between them.

"Just the man I was looking to find."

Tony offered the joint, and Lionel reflexively accepted. Lionel's recent employment interrupted his smoking regimen, so even a few hours without a hit meant brain fog, fatigue, headaches, and general depletion. His body still produced mucus consistent with constant smoking, which gathered in his eyes and clouded his vision. The joint cleared his muddled thoughts and woke him up, but his right eye became further irritated and inflamed with goop.

"You showing up here the other day was like a cosmic event."

"Word."

"No 'word.' You were trying to pass your problems off on me."

"I came to the wrong house," said Lionel, showing Tony the address on his palm. "I'll load everything up and get out of here."

"No, no, no. Not until I fill you in on where I'm at with this. You coming here was one in a series of synchronicities that I was praying for only moments before you arrived." Lionel frowned. "Security saw your car and figured you were coming from my lawyer. His paralegal drops stuff off here in the same model Lexus you drove up in. Synchronicity Number One. And it just so happened that you were also dropping off legal documents, just like his paralegal. Synchronicity Number Two. So I thought that I was getting sued, but when I read through the documents, I could only find stuff about you. That's when I ran into Synchronicity Number Three."

"Wait." Lionel stopped itching his closed right eye with his knuckle. "What about me?"

"Your legal situation."

Ringing started in Lionel's ears.

"In those boxes?"

Tony widened his eyes. "Yeah. Everywhere. It says Lionel Lancet lawsuit, Lionel Lancet tax fraud. I would add Lionel Lancet passing his problems off on somebody else. Lawsuits don't work like that. You can't just drop it off at somebody's house. I ought to sue you for that. Just for scaring the shit out of me."

Adrenaline plumed in Lionel's chest and ignited his high with the irrational notion that everything around him became a hot surface. As he ran his clammy palms against the fabric of his pants, a cluster of thoughts he couldn't follow blossomed at the center of his head, each darting off and fizzling out like a drip of water on a stove. Something inside of him did a full somersault.

It might have been the glow of the grow lights against the mist or the goop in his eyes, but each object around him seemed to shine out of itself from some withdrawn source. Whatever it was inside of him that moved around wanted out. It wanted to swim to the source of the objects in the greenhouse, perfectly content to leave him behind. It took all of his courage to burst through an invisible wall he erected that prevented him from speaking.

"Where are they?" said Lionel, a bit too forcefully.

Tony's hand was bringing the joint to his lips, but it stopped. He turned his head slowly to look at Lionel.

"I will not be intimidated in my own greenhouse."

Lionel coughed like he was choking. "No... breathing gets hard when I freak out." He gagged, and Tony recoiled.

"Don't puke on the inventory."

Tony ushered Lionel out of the greenhouse.

When they reached the driveway, Marcus finished stacking Lionel's boxes on the stone landing outside the front door. As Lionel approached the stack, he gave no indication that his equilibrium see-sawed tauntingly. He bent down to withdraw a few papers from his delivery, and sure enough, "Lionel Lancet" was ubiquitous in the maelstrom of legal terms and dollar amounts written in red. It looked like he was reading, but his thundering heartbeat pulsed into his vision, subsuming the rest of the words on the page into an unintelligible wash.

The day surrounded him with sauna heat that entered his nose, dry and raw, but his entire body trembled as he inelegantly filed the papers back into the box and replaced the cardboard lid. The words he failed to read stained his eyes, and the colors in the space around him filtered through dancing letters. He attempted to carry a box to his car, but the slight exertion broke him, putting him on all fours, where he whimpered and clawed at his uncooperative buttons, and at last he pushed himself back on his knees and tore his shirt in half.

His interior darted about, amounting to not quite an out-of-body experience, but a this-side-of-his-body then that-side-of-his-body escape attempt like a scared animal trapped in a sack. The fluid in his ears was telling him he was leaning too far one way, but he wasn't sure which way that was, and whichever way was right didn't agree with where the ground and sky were. Through it all, he was falling in place, perceiving himself and Tony and the space around him with motion lines, surging through time, not as objects with mass and weight, but as symbols that signified presence without depth, mere shapes in his vision that he could not interpret.

Tony watched in disbelief, backed away as if he were about to get splashed. The sweat pouring from Lionel made that not unlikely. As the episode started to subside and his breathing normalized, Lionel trained his eyes on the ground. He adjusted a box on the stack as casually as he could.

"Sorry," said Lionel. "P-panic attacks."

Tony slipped into the house, and after a short while he returned with a folded dashiki in black and gold. He held it out to Lionel.

"Here. You can't go back to work like that."

After a moment of consideration, keeping his eyes down, Lionel accepted the shirt and seated himself on the bottom step of the landing. The sun had heated the stone, and it warmed his butt pleasantly. With great effort, he slipped out of the torn shirt and into the dashiki. Its loose fit was spacious and comfortable. He rested his elbow on his knee and his chin on his hand, taking in grounds that extended far in front of him.

Tony cleared his throat.

"I thought you went inside," said Lionel. "I'll go."

"Hold up." Tony sat down next to Lionel. "See, from where I'm at... This is a...*n event*. Like, a true... It's like it fell out of the sky. The day you came here, I was ready to give up. I wanted to end it all. And I prayed. I asked God for a sign. And you showed up just like that. Synchronicity Number Three."

"So?"

"So to pay me back for scaring the shit out of me, you could hook me up with Adhikashara." Lionel looked at him blankly. "That's exactly the inspiration I need. If I can get in touch with what holds the ultimate power in my life, I'll be unstoppable. I'm supposed to direct. Actual film. I'm done watching people fuck. Like, would an *Agile Twinks IV* really say anything we didn't cover in *Agile Twinks I* through *III*?"

"I don't know what that is."

"*Agile Twinks*? If you're not watching gay porn, you wouldn't have seen it. I'm not gay myself, but business is business. And gymnastics is for everyone."

"I mean, I don't have anything to give you."

"Yes, you do. Adhikashara. I might be saying it wrong, but I know all about it. You hook me up, and we're good. Don't play dumb. I read those documents."

"I haven't. I barely know about the lawsuit."

"Your lawyer will figure it out. They've got strategies for this kind of thing."

"I don't have a lawyer."

"That's bold," said Tony. "Let me give you Blackwell and Finkbiner's number. They're great with criminals."

"Why did Damian have those boxes?"

"Damian?"

"It doesn't fucking matter," said Lionel with a defeated sigh. Although his episode passed, his heartbeat remained elevated at the thought of mustering a pathetic, feeble confrontation and Damian dismissing it without moving his expressionless, plastic face.

"How about we arrange a time for you to come back? I'll clear my schedule." Tony scrolled through his phone.

"I can't. I don't have…"

"Adhikashara."

"I don't know what that is. I have to leave." Lionel tried and failed to pick up a box. "Could you have someone take these to the car for me?"

Tony got Marcus to load the boxes into the trunk, and Lionel stood watching him as Tony changed his bargaining tactic.

"You owe me."

"I said I was sorry."

"You're Lionel Lancet, right?"

"Yes."

"The president of the Fiduciary Royal... That foundation?"

Lionel stopped and turned back to him.

"Oh, that's right. I completely forgot about that."

"How crazy is your life?"

Lionel had nothing left to say. He got in his car, and Tony peered through the driver's side window.

"I'll pay you."

"I don't know what it is! I don't have it." Lionel put on his seatbelt and lowered the window. "Seriously, Tony. I didn't even know what was in those boxes until ten minutes ago. I don't know what you want from me."

"Adhik—"

"I don't know what that is!" Lionel thought he expressed exasperation, but Tony's almost fearful reaction told him it was something else.

"You could just say no," said Tony, looking away, a little hurt. "It's just a little communication. But I would like to know why you won't sell me any. I'm a good guy, Lionel."

"I don't sell anything."

"I can tell when I'm being disrespected," said Tony. "I've got to ask though. What's it like?"

"I don't know."

"Don't do your own product. Respect." Tony lit another joint. "I'll pay you double your usual price." Lionel had stopped answering him. "I'll give you a hundred thousand dollars." Marcus finished loading the boxes into Lionel's trunk and closed it. "Lionel, I gave you the shirt off my back."

"I mean, you got it from inside..."

"It's the principle!"

"Do you want it back? It's a nice shirt."

"Keep it. If you change your mind, you know where to find me."

Lionel started to roll down the driveway, and he rolled up his window. Joint in hand, Tony stood shaking his head as Lionel's car passed through the wrought-iron gate.

Stopping in front of the house next door, Lionel looked down at his palm: 446 Hillcrest Drive. Framed in the passenger window, 446 was inlaid in stone on the column next to the security gate. Barely visible between the hedges, in the center of the lawn, standing on one foot, ten arms spread out every which way, one of which was holding a severed head, was a statue of the Hindu goddess Kali. Lionel craned his neck, squinting, to see through the hedges, and upon making out the statue, he tilted his head to the side with a horrified look on his face. He floored the gas as though Kali might come alive and chase him. She stayed put, but a car rounded the corner and followed him.

Chapter 12

Lionel's high set with the sun, and a dull afterglow remained as cool night air crept onto the grounds of the Hotel Bellehaven. He lay spread out on his bed as if he were being crucified in a lazy X, his eyes staring unfocused beneath the slowly spinning fan. His anxious fantasies that soared toward the most sinister conclusions now petered out before gaining any traction.

The contents of the boxes he was supposed to deliver certainly meant something, and so did the discovery that Damian was involved, but Lionel had been too high to determine just what that was. He reasoned it could be terrible, but it could also be harmless. It could go either way. Good or bad. Fifty-fifty. Were positive and negative outcomes equally distributed in the universe? Dawkins probably wouldn't have liked that logic, but the possibility eased Lionel's mind during the drive to his villa.

The car tailing him abandoned its pursuit before the 405, and his racing thoughts dissipated on the slow crawl south to the 10, where he finally achieved panic fatigue. The evidence lay in the boxes in his trunk, and until he read the documents, there was no proof that anything was amiss.

Unable to avoid it any longer, he sat up in his bed, resolving himself to confront the legal documents and accept whatever they told him.

He sneaked back and forth between his car and the villa's adobe-enclosed porch, unloading the boxes. More than once he paused to bend over and catch his breath. As the propane fire heated the fake logs in the fireplace and warmed the area around his wicker chair, he withdrew the papers and prepared himself to investigate the evidence, reminding himself to focus only on the facts.

This proved immediately to be boring. He was emotionally depleted, his brain felt raw, and in spite of the fire, he shivered in his dashiki. A joint and a blanket were necessary if this was going to work. When he went inside, the cigars he took from his grandfather's house gave him an idea: he was going to roll a blunt.

Lionel parted the cigar's brown wrapping with his thumbs and emptied the expensive tobacco into the toilet. He brought the wrapping to his nose and smelled its musk. Even as an experienced smoker, he was slightly nervous about the size of the blunt. Blunts were notorious for sending people beyond the horizon, but that was just where Lionel decided he needed to go. After grinding more weed than usual, he poured it into the empty cigar and slathered saliva on the edges to seal it.

With a blanket wrapped around him, he got thoroughly obliterated and managed to return to his wicker chair, ready to absorb legal jargon and financial data. While the documents were mostly comprised of English sentences (with the exception of photocopied text written in symbols Lionel had never seen before), it might as well have been an alien language sent to earth to twist his already crooked sense of reality into a pretzel. The only words he recognized were his name and President of the Fiduciary Royalties Association for United Donors.

One stack at a time, he withdrew papers, failed to understand their contents, and tossed them to the side. This went on until he came across the word Adhikashara. It was in a stapled packet of papers with a hand-written account penned by his grandfather that read as follows:

The time has come to put to print the apparent "effects" of Adhikashara, if it's fair to call them that, given their mysterious capacity to breakdown one's concept of before and after, cause and effect, and just about every other construct with which we delude ourselves in order to keep on an even keel in our awakening into form as bipedal moss that has grown like a thatch whose strands of straw insist on a separation between themselves and the unbroken field of grass from which they were raised.

Lionel looked up, exhausted. He reread the sentence several times, and eventually decided to ignore everything after "...*the 'effects' of Adhikashara...* " He took a deep breath and continued reading.

It would be impossible to avoid language's capacity to strip the experience away from the communication thereof, pounding it into metal sheets and beams that structure a hollow dwelling, a poor artifice of the cave that housed the raw materials that we might have been better off by staying in, saving ourselves the headache of advancing... But as a misguided, upwardly mobile troglodyte whose constructed house is not without luxuries afforded by the modern world, I cannot descend into the past in an embodied form any more than I can share this experience in the totality it deserves. However, for the sake of shedding dim light into a black hole that might swallow it anyway, I'll give it my best.

Through sheer accident, we stumbled upon Adhikashara, and it was only after extensive experimentation that we were able to settle on a uniform "effect" for those who partake in this psychedelic eucharist which transubstantiates molecules into a looking glass that reliably shows that which holds the ultimate power in the user's life.

The open-endedness of this claim isn't lost on me, and it is far from my interest to explain the experience with any rigor or science, whose status as a target for my contempt should be well known. However, the experience, I have found, is replicable, which might please the more rigid-minded.

I can only ask that you accept my word and account of others' experiences as at least compelling enough to inspire further research, first or secondhand, though it should be obvious by now which of the two ordinal hands I recommend.

With this exhaustive preamble out of the way, I would like to share an account of my own experience with Adhikashara, but keep in mind that no inference should be made about a similar experience. That which holds power over me might not track to the experiences of others.

After a single drink of Adhikashara, I sat on the cliffside porch in my home, awaiting transcendence of one kind or another, with usual tingly bodily sensations and a warmth in my core that radiated outward until it began to thrum the point at the center of my head—not a physical point at all, but a locus where my sense of self resided—and bring to it a slight pulse that unraveled it and sent "Me" or whatever was left of me to the surrounding sounds, the breeze, the pleasant wash of the tide which was just out of view.

There was nothing to validate my experience because the colors and shapes didn't appear to me in my formlessness, but I was not blind any more than dust is blind. Sight was simply not applicable. A change took hold, but to say that I manifested in various media, which is the state I found myself in, falsely implies that I had a choice. But I was no more in control than the trickling sound from running water is about its arrival into the aural field. For there I was birthed out of a faucet, reverberating within the sink, and meshed with the gargles from its swirling into the drain. I became the cracking sound in the chipped graphite of a pencil dragged across construction paper, and even the faint hiss from the steam rising from a crockpot full of stew. I'm aware it might be quickly dismissed as a projection of my form onto the shapelessness of sound...

It would take a less strict interpretation of objects and the material world to mind my presence in a way that would make me feel looked at, but given the common resistance to such soft interpretation of the real, I can only say that I continued braiding myself or rather, I was being braided into the waves of the sound of the world in relative secrecy, further swept away by the forces I took to be my will, but they were truly hugely different from that. It was then (or there? or neither?) that I discovered the "source" of the ultimate power in my life, and it caught me by surprise: sound, music, the disembodied spirit of the universe that compensates for all of the world's failure to show us the core of anything. For sight can offer only a glimpse of a surface, and only the surface that's facing us at that.

The soul of any object is made known through sound, of dropping a book on the floor, of a door slammed shut, or of a booming horn from the passing fairy on its way to Catalina. As for ourselves, it's the emotional intonation of our speech and not its denotation that shares our soul. We might provide clearer access to our interiors through chanting the sacred

Om, and our music that pours forth is the interior laid to bare as we're beset by rote objects and mitigated phenomena that leave no other recourse than to pattern our animals cries into melodies, our one authentic stance against the far-reaching expanse that would resist any attempt of ours to codify it, and so too shows more clearly what holds power over me: Vibrations—

Lionel looked up at once. "Vibes?" said Lionel. "Fucking *vibes?*" Blowing air through his pursed lips, he got up and threw the paper into the fire, the edges curling as they burned, reducing Art's account of the ultimate power in his life to a crumpled ball of cinders. He faced the boxes with his hands on his hips, deciding to roll another blunt before burning the rest of the documents.

Part II
Interrogations

Chapter 13

A knock came at the door, and Lionel's eyes opened, unfocused and bloodshot. He slept through the day, and the darkness outside of his window disoriented his sense of time. If he refused to answer the door, maybe whoever knocked would go away. If he refused to answer it, maybe whoever knocked wouldn't exist. He didn't believe this per se, but it was a comforting thought. Another knock. As if to confirm his rationalism to himself, he rose to answer it.

It was a bellboy with a manilla envelope in his hands.

"Mail for you, sir."

Lionel, thoroughly put upon by having to engage with a human, gave an unconvincing smile, grabbed the envelope, and shut the door in the bellboy's face. He fell heavily into the couch, and after an extended moment of blinking and staring into space, he opened the envelope, revealing another subpoena, this one for a deposition. He had to look up what that was, and his stomach sank.

Dark fantasies consumed him: working for the rest of his life to repay debts that he did not know the source of, turning into a ghostly presence, an absence, guests coming and going, treating him as a permanent fixture in the hotel. Any lasting relationship with anyone, especially Tomiina, would be impossible. Her family wouldn't stay at the hotel forever.

Lionel returned to his bedroom and prepared a blunt out of another one of his grandfather's cigars. He smoked and began watching Milo Yiannopoulos debate a feminist in a college classroom, but there was another knock at the door. Leaving the laptop on his bed and the burning blunt on his nightstand, he rose to answer the door. It was Tomiina, wearing a white nightgown and curlers in her hair. Slung over her shoulder was an overnight bag. Even if he were sober, Lionel would have given the same open-mouthed stare. Unprompted, Tomiina let herself in, and he immediately got an erection.

She sat on the couch in his living room, taking in his place with slight nods, and her nostrils flared at the smell from his blunt. Lionel sat next to her and waited for her to initiate the conversation, sex, or a confession that she never liked him and that all of this was a ruse. The lingering silence took away his breath, and the tension in his chest swelled toward an unknown point that would break him unless he could bring himself to do anything at all. Her eyes drifted to the subpoena.

Suddenly inspired, Tomiina slapped her hands down on her thighs. At the sound of contact, adrenaline fluttered in him.

Her inspiration was to make drinks. She withdrew a metal cocktail shaker and a drawstring bag of bitters from her overnight bag and got to work in the kitchen.

Lionel feigned ease with his hands behind his head and his legs crossed. Shaking ice in the cocktail shaker interrupted him just as his mouth opened to start a conversation. He pursed his lips together.

Tomiina returned with the drinks which she garnished with tiny umbrellas. They sat in silence until she gestured that they both drink.

"Would you like to receive a Tarot reading?" She brought out a deck of Rider-Waite tarot cards from her overnight bag and shook the box at him playfully.

"Is that like psychic stuff?"

"No." Tomiina rose and seated herself on the floor on the opposite side of the coffee table.

"I don't think I want to play," said Lionel, pretending to be distracted with something on his fingernails.

"It's not a game. Haven't you ever gotten a reading?"

"I don't believe in that stuff."

"What stuff?"

"Tarot cards, magic. Lucky rocks."

"This is different. I think a one-card reading would be good for a beginner."

She set the deck down on the coffee table and dragged a spread of cards into an arc with one swift motion. Pleased with herself, she put her hands down behind the spread. "We're going to see what's looming in your subconscious."

"I doubt there's much."

"You wouldn't know. It's *sub*conscious."

"I guess. But you know... I don't really have any looming..."

"Baggage? Repression? Blocked chakras?"

"I wouldn't say it like that, but yeah." Even the slight confrontation of simply stating his diverging opinion was a taxing ordeal. He would have to save his energy in case she pounced on him for sex, which seemed likely to him. The nightgown, the curlers, the overnight bag, all of this was evidence that indicated a sleepover. He sat up and opened himself to the room.

"Think of a question or an intention or an issue that has been bugging you, an uncertainty about your life."

"How did Damian get my legal documents?"

Tomiina frowned. "'How' questions aren't really the best. Make it about you."

"Something is up. He's trying to do something... bad. Or wrong. To me."

"Like what?"

"That's just it. I don't know. But it's definitely really bad. Possibly."

"Why don't you pick a question that doesn't have so many assumptions attached to it?"

"He was sending my documents all over town. That's a fact."

"What did he say when you asked him about it?"

"I didn't. I didn't want to let him know that I know what he's up to. But his reaction when he found out that I brought them to the wrong house gave the whole thing away."

"Gave what away?"

"The thing he's trying to do to me. You should have seen his face. I mean, his face didn't move much. But you could just tell that whatever he's doing, it's serious."

"Okay, whatever. Pick a question or intention that isn't about Damian. It has to be about you."

"That's definitely the biggest one on my mind. Okay, how about... what's in store for me... in relation to Damian's plan?"

"Wave your hand over the cards... not that fast... close your eyes... and when you feel compelled, put your hand down and select a card."

"I don't really feel anything. Should I just pick a random card?"

"No. You should feel for something."

"But how do I know if I actually feel something or if I just think I do?"

"Close your eyes!"

"Okay, this one. But I just kinda picked."

"Oh, very interesting."

"What? Did I pick right?"

"You can open your eyes."

Slowly, she set the card Lionel picked on the table. It depicted an armored, flag-wielding skeleton riding on a pale horse, towering over a bishop and commoners who seemed to plead for their lives. Beneath the horse lay a dead king, his crown off his head. At the bottom of the card was the word Death.

Lionel frowned.

"Death isn't necessarily bad. It can mean an old you is dying away to make way for the new. It can be rebirth. And notice the bishop, king, and the commoners. Death comes for all of them alike. So that means your rebirth is inevitable."

"I don't know how you came up with that."

"It comes with experience."

"What does my death have to do with Damian?"

"Death or rebirth. It can also mean to let go. Do you want to draw a clarification card?"

"Death seems pretty clear." Lionel closed his eyes, waving his hands over the spread-out cards and selected a card when he felt compelled. Tomiina turned it over.

"The Five of Cups reversed. Interesting."

"Interesting good? Or interesting bad?"

"Look at the picture. It's a guy standing with three fallen cups in front of him, and two upright cups behind him. He's standing next to a river, and there's a bridge over it that leads to a castle."

"So I'm going to die with cups by a river?"

"If it's right side up, you are focusing on the spilled cups, but you don't notice the full, standing cups behind you. So you would need to stop focusing on your losses, and focus on what you have in order to move forward to cross the bridge over the river and get to the castle. But since it is reversed, it means that it might behoove you to look into the past. You might need closure or forgiveness before you can get to the castle. You might need to come to terms with the influence of your past, your family, or your ancestors. Does that resonate with you?"

"You said the Death card told me to let go, and this one says to look into the past. That's the exact opposite."

"Not necessarily. Sometimes things that are opposites can be the same."

Lionel blinked, overwhelmed by the myriad potential objections he could voice. "How do you know what the card means?"

"It's right on the card."

"Where?"

"The picture. Look at it."

"That picture doesn't say that."

"Of course it does. Look at it."

"That's just your interpretation."

"*Look* at it!"

"I am looking at it! And I could say that it's about a guy who got drunk by a river, and he can't drink anymore, so he doesn't get into the last 2 cups, and he's hanging his head because the alcohol is getting to him, and the river is in his way, so he's realizing that he is too drunk to walk home and he has to sleep on the river bank tonight."

"That would be a terrible interpretation."

"There are infinite ways to interpret this."

"Incorrect. If I looked at the Five of Cups and said it as a warning about an alien invasion, that would be a stupid, bad, incorrect interpretation."

"How do you know it's not about an alien invention? Were you there when whoever drew the cards?"

"You drew the cards. So yes."

"No, the guy who drew the pictures. How do you know what he intended?"

"It doesn't matter what she intended. It was a she, by the way."

"Do you believe that?"

"Of course! It's well documented that the illustrations were done by Pamela Colman Smith."

"No. Do you believe that it doesn't matter what she intended?"

"It doesn't change what she drew. Read the drawing. Is that a man?"

"Yes."

"Is it an apple?'

"No."

"Is it a football?"

"No."

"What is it?"

"It's a man."

"And what's he doing?"

"He's looking at three spilled cups."

"And what's behind him?"

"Two cups."

"Are they spilled?"

"No."

"And what's that?"

"A river."

"Is it a pizza?"

"No."

"Is it a candelabra?"

"No."

"It's a river. And that's a bridge. And that's a castle. And the Five of Cups means you need to stop focusing on your spilled cups to notice your full ones, so you can cross the bridge over the river and get to the castle." Tomiina threw the card on the table.

"But you said the Death card was open to interpretation, and this one is just set in stone?"

"That's the thing about interpreting the cards, you have to have the insider knowledge that comes from experience. It's *in*sider knowledge, that's why it's *in*terpretation."

"That can't be right."

Tomiina leaned over the table without breaking eye contact. A pleasant, aching sensation appeared in Lionel's gut, and he froze as she kissed him softly, which released the ache and induced a drunken wistfulness in him. She pulled away as he leaned in for more and looked at her as if she had denied him something, which she ignored, sipping her drink.

Lionel followed suit, taking a hardy gulp.

"Don't read into it."

Lionel tried to stifle a smirk, simultaneously annoyed, smitten, turned on, and a little sleepy now. He broke eye contact and gazed out the window, but it was too dark to see anything outside.

"Okay, but the Five of Cups was reversed. So... flipping a picture upside down makes it mean the opposite of what it says? That is so irrational."

"You're being contrary, and it's getting really annoying."

"It's just that, logically, this seems delusional and irrational. And it seems like you've been... forceful... with your beliefs since we've been involved."

This hit her like a bolt of lightning. Her mouth hung open. "Involved? Is that what you think this is? You never communicated any of that to me, so you have no right to get mad and expect me to feel guilty. Honestly, Lionel, did you really think you even had a chance?"

Lionel cowered, his mind blank. Tomiina stood and turned away from him to fume. With wide eyes, he searched for anything to say. She whipped back around quickly. Something she saw in his bedroom transformed her rage into disgust.

"Milo Yiannopoulos? Seriously?"

His laptop lay open on his bed.

"Yeah?"

"You are... *Ugh.*"

"He's entertaining. I don't really believe what he says. Not all of it, anyway. You should see what's happening on college campuses."

Tomiina put the cards away hurriedly. Lionel rose to stop her.

"You—"

"Oh, so it's all my fault? Where do *you* fit into all of this, Lionel? I want to hear that part."

"I didn't even do anything."

"What a surprise? Lionel: sitting there doing nothing at all."

"Please stay."

"Stay? You thought that I was going to stay? You are unbelievable. I'm staying at a friend's place tonight."

"Is it a guy?"

"Good night, Lionel."

"Who is it?"

"My friend Jarrod."

"I'm sorry."

"Goodbye, Lionel,"

The words sounded boxy as if Tomiina spoke with her hand cupped against his ear. Perhaps the fluid in his ears shifted. She pushed past him and left.

His laptop ruined everything for him. Groaning, he stomped into his room and slammed it shut. Collapsing face down on his bed and bellowing into his pillow seemed like the only path forward. After a moment, he pivoted to reach for the blunt that he left on the nightstand. He lit it up, but it didn't make him feel better.

Seeking the comfort of YouTube, he opened his laptop and discovered a crack that ran diagonally across the screen. He threw his head back against the headboard of his bed and had a long moment to himself with his eyes closed.

He wanted to push the argument out of his head, but something inside of him kept it going. Tomiina saw a whole story in the simple pictures on the tarot cards. Why was she so willing to mix her projections with the facts? It was as though truth for her was a matter of attaching her opinions to reality. There was a reason that scientists leave opinions out of their work. Opinions are attached to emotions, and emotions cloud your judgment. They make you believe what you want to be true instead of what is true.

Tomiina saw a value-judgment in everything like it was inscribed in every object. Certainly, Lionel had opinions of his own somewhere deep down, but he didn't let these distract from the facts. He considered his value-judgments as nothing more than empty words hovering over the objects they referred to. Lionel was no linguist, but he felt it was safe to assume that the word "interpretation" had nothing to do with the word "insider." If she took liberties with her words, why was she so offended by Milo's speech?

His laptop still worked in spite of the damage. Milo Yiannopoulos videos filled his recommendations, and clicked on a video titled "Milo Yiannopoulos & Rebecca Reid: 'Have We Reached an Age of Gender Equality?'" He watched passively, his attention split between the screen and his blunt. But one argument of Milo's piqued his interest:

> There is some reason to suppose there is an advantage to being a man in certain subjects, there's a reason to suppose that gender essentialism, biological determinism, whatever you want to call it, the fact that there are male brains and female brains, may indeed have some basis in science.

Chapter 14

The etiquette of proving a case, granting the most charitable interpretation to opponents' arguments, interested Melanie Bobbers in law school, when she thought justice, morality, and the whole world for that matter were perfectly navigable through reason alone. Determining guilt or innocence was a matter of deduction. This made sense in the perspective of a student who dealt with theoretical cases where there was no devil in the details and landmark cases on which the verdicts were already decided.

Melanie quickly learned that careful rhetoric and fairness mapped poorly onto the real world. None of her opponents felt compelled to stick to any consistent story at all. And their language was anything but reasonable. The game they played included argumentation as only a narrow portion of their available moves, favoring tactics more closely resembling those of the animal kingdom. Exoneration was fought for and won or lost. The only thing they proved was the moral limits of their opponents and their own lack thereof as they sat across from her, smirking, bending the truth and the world around them.

Melanie had to learn to let arguments serve her scratching and clawing at predators, instead of trying to piece her offensive neatly into a proof. Before long, she saw fair play as only her attempt to validate herself before powerful men, and eventually, before herself. Just as they saw their entitlement to do as they pleased as a self-evident right, she began to see her desire to defeat them as an impulse that required no explanation. Besides, she didn't want to convince them they were guilty. She wanted to send them to jail.

Lionel was deposed at Melanie's office in Highland Park, a small brick loft above a coffee shop with hip, faded signage. The inside was designed with industrial piping and Edison light bulbs. Lionel squirmed throughout the drive across town.

Melanie wore a brace around her neck and a bandage on her left cheek, which crinkled as she spoke. She had her left canine tooth replaced, but the swelling had yet to subside, making her face asymmetrical. A private security guard stood in the corner, eyeing Lionel.

Lionel sat across from Melanie, avoiding eye contact with the camera that she set up too close to him. He wore a pink, paisley dress shirt that Tomiina sent to his room, and his perspiration already saturated the fabric under the sleeves. The light trained on him made matters worse. Lionel's bottom lip gave away his uncertainty that he would emerge from the deposition in one piece.

Melanie took her time laying out her binders and reams of paper which composed her case against him, and once she finished, the court reporter swore him in, and she began.

MELANIE BOBBERS, State Bar No. 1360441
5703½ Figueroa Street
Los Angeles, California 90042-4201
Telephone: (323)555-7431
Facsimile: (323)555-7300

THE UNITED STATES   Case No. BC4351893
                Plaintiff
     vs.

LIONEL LANCET
                Defendant

SUPERIOR COURT OF THE STATE OF CALIFORNIA

COUNTY OF LOS ANGELES

            DEPOSITION OF LIONEL LANCET,
the defendant herein, taken on behalf of the
Plaintiffs at 10:23 A.M., Thursday, July 21,
2016, at 5703½ Figueroa Street, Los Angeles,
California, before Joella Danforth, C&R 2222,
rpr, pursuant to Notice.

Q. Please state your name for the record.

A. Lionel Lancet.

Q. I want to make sure you know your role today. Have you ever been deposed before?

A. No.

Q. How this works is that I'm going to ask you questions, and we need full answers, so no 'uh-huh' or 'uh-uh' because those can be ambiguous in writing. For the sake of our court reporter, please give full answers. Understand?

A. Uh-huh.

Q. I'm going to need a full answer.

A. Yes. Fair. Yes, that sounds fair.

Q. Is your foundation, the Fiduciary Royalties Association for United Donors, currently active?

A. Not that I know of. I wouldn't call it my foundation.

Q. Do you deny that your foundation is still active?

A. I don't deny it. I don't know.

Q. You say that it's not your foundation, but these documents demonstrate the opposite. Could you please read who is listed as president?

A. I didn't agree to that. I didn't even know about it.

Q. Yes, but would you please read into the record who is listed as president?

A. I'm not sure I should.

Q. Let the record reflect that Lionel became hostile in refusing to admit that he's president.

A. I didn't get hostile.

Q. Mr. Lancet, please quit making that menacing face… And, for the record, Lionel Lancet is the name listed as President.

Q. Would you consider yourself a strong person?

A. Like, physically?

Q. Like, strong-willed.

A. Uh… maybe. Yeah. Yes. Well… I'm not sure.

Q. Do you like to have the upper hand in your relationships?

A. I don't think so.

Q. Does it make you feel strong to take advantage of weaker people?

A. I don't. If anything, it feels like people take advantage of me. By the way, I have some suspicions about my boss. Do you happen to know someone named-

Q. Do you think that you have any legal responsibilities as president of your foundation?

A. Yes. I mean, no. I was not president. And I'm not now.

Q. Did you at any point in your role as president of your foundation try to diminish or disguise your legal responsibilities?

A. I never did anything as president.

Q. Would you be willing to sign this document?

A. I don't know what this is.

Q. Is it fair to say it's printed clearly and legibly?

A. Yeah, but—

Q. Are you refusing to read the document?

A. I guess I am.

Q. Fine. I'll read it. 'I, Lionel Lancet, President of the Fiduciary Royalties

Association for United Donors, could have prevented the harmful actions of my foundation, including its misappropriation of funds, contributions to problematic conservative causes, and refusal to pay taxes. I could have been more attentive to the systemic consequences of my actions and the legal and material implications for the large swaths of people affected.' Are you willing to sign this document?

A. No.

Q. Why not?

A. I'm- I don't think I was a part of any of that. I didn't even know I was in the foundation. And I don't know what they did. What even happened? Who got hurt? Like, how do you know that it's this big thing? It sounds like you're making a lot of assumptions, and maybe shit just happens and you're connecting dots where there aren't any. It's a delusion.

Q. Is it fair to say you usually let other people push you around?

A. I don't let them. They just do it anyway.

Q. Do you get the feeling that everyone is against you?

A. Sometimes, I guess.

Q. Does it annoy you when people criticize you?

A. Doesn't it annoy everyone?

Q. I'll ask the questions here. Do you believe that you are above criticism?

A. No.

Q. Should everyone be nice to you?

A. Within reason, I guess. Everyone should be nice to everybody.

Q. How would you describe your relationship with your mother?

A. I don't know.

Q. Estranged?

A. I guess.

Q. Now, you and I have met before when I served you with a subpoena, and you told me about your mother. Could you, for the record, tell me what you told me then?

A. I don't remember.

Q. Not about where she went?

A. Oh yeah. She left when I was thirteen.

Q. Do you keep in contact with her?

A. Not really. She sends me cards from Spain occasionally.

Q. Spain? That's right. I believe you said she ran away with a bullfighter. That's quite a profession. Are you sure he was a bullfighter?

A. Pretty sure.

Q. Did you ever see him fight a bull?

A. No. That's just what my dad told me. She ran away with a bullfighter.

Q. Right. To what degree was your mother involved with your foundation?

A. I don't know.

Q. Do you deny that she was involved?

A. I really don't know.

Q. Are you attempting to win back your mother's love that has been absent since your early adolescence?

A. No.

Q. Do you have a girlfriend, Lionel?

A. No.

Q. Do you know a young woman named Tomiina Deatherage?

A. Yes.

Q. How would you describe your relationship with her?

A. She's really great. But also annoying.

Q. That's a loaded answer. Could you expound?

A. I think she likes me. But I'm not sure.

Q. Would you say it's an intimate relationship?

A. Not really.

Q. Another loaded answer.

A. I mean, we kissed once, but I think she kissed me to prove a point.

Q. Odd.

A. Is that a question?

Q. Could you describe Tomiina?

A. Like, what she looks like?

Q. You immediately assume it's about her appearance. What does she do for a living?

A. She's a famous actress.

Q. Yes, she is, isn't she? Don't you think it's odd that she would be interested in you?

A. I don't know what you mean.

Q. What does she like about you?

A. She said she likes how I'm not a tryhard.

Q. But wouldn't you say it seems like an odd match?

A. Uh-huh.

Q. I'm sorry, I'll need a full answer.

A. Yes.

Q. Are you a famous person?

A. No.

Q. Are you talented?

A. At what?

Q. Anything?

A. I like ideas. Does that count?

Q. Don't famous people usually date other famous people?

A. I don't really know.

Q. Could you guess as to whether famous people usually date other famous people?

A. That seems reasonable.

Q. Outside of her career, could you describe the kind of person she is?

A. She likes weird stuff.

Q. Like what?

A. Crystals and magic and stuff.

Q. Like, magic tricks?

A. Tarot cards. Woo-woo stuff.

Q. Is she religious?

A. Probably. She probably doesn't like Christianity, but probably Buddhism or something like that.

Q. Are you a religious person?

A. No. Religion is a—

Q. Do you control the religious aspects of your foundation?

A. I don't know anything about the foundation. And if I did, I definitely wouldn't have anything to do with whatever religious stuff we do. They do, I mean.

Q. Someone else in the foundation then?

A. Someone else what?

Q. Perhaps someone else in the foundation carries out the religious rituals?

A. Rituals? Like church?

Q. Is Tomiina in charge of the rituals?

A. She isn't in the foundation.

Q. Is Eli Deatherage in charge of the rituals?

A. Are you saying… Wait, was he involved in all of this?

Q. Eli Deatherage is on the board of the Hotel Bellehaven, one of many business interests in common with your grandfather. This can't be news to you.

A. I… excuse me. Just got…

Q. Did you organize an attempt on my life? Did you order the ritual sacrifice on me? Are there other victims? Now is the time to come clean, Lionel. They'll get rid of you the moment they don't need you anymore. I have no further questions. Could you strike that last part, please?

Lionel's arms and legs hung limply off the chair as if someone dropped him there, and nothing in the room was included in the scope of his unfocused, drifting eyes. He had gone white. The court reporter scrolled through the transcript, and Melanie busied herself with her papers without concealing the smile that spread across her swollen face.

"Thank you for your time, Mr. Lancet," said Melanie without looking up. As Lionel rose and staggered toward the exit, she positioned herself in front of the camera. "The only thing Lionel Lancet managed to sacrifice today was his reputation." She did a second take as he walked down the stairs. He had to lean on the railing for support.

Chapter 15

Golden hour glowed through the window in Lionel's living room, replacing the pale white light of the day, and seagulls hovered in place against the wind drafts. A suitcase propped open the front door, and a pile of towels and robes he intended to steal lay in a pile in his bedroom. The pink paisley dress shirt he wore to the deposition hung out of the kitchen trash can with a tear down the front. Several buttons were missing.

Lionel's eyes were wide the entire drive to his villa in spite of the low sun shining in his face. A cyclist swerved at the last moment to avoid getting plowed, and he waved absently to apologize. The odometer read 90 mph after he rounded the curve where the 10 turned into the PCH in Santa Monica.

His interior simmered as he packed his belongings into the trunk and backseat of his car. What before was the promise of immediate escape was now a slow evaporation of whatever he harbored inside. He attempted to cry to urge the feeling out of its aggravated potential, but it maintained its slow effusive burn.

All Melanie revealed or at least implied about Tomiina pointed toward some ulterior motive. Lionel concluded that it was to sacrifice him in a religious ritual. The insecurity that undergirded his interactions with her, Lionel figured, were an expression of his inadequacy, but now it seemed clear that her freedom and confidence, which he could never match, were dangerous, potentially lethal. He overlooked any threat because her company provided an upshot for the lonely, stoned existence he was drifting through. But the warning signs were there, evidence of something sinister.

His resentment for Tomiina quickly became resentment toward himself, for getting involved with her, for believing he was worthy of a woman that beautiful, for thinking that something about himself transcended his hideous body and his ugly face. Her feminine allure distracted him from these facts. Instead, fanciful narratives about the two of them in love danced in his head. She tricked him into believing that there was some higher version of himself lurking inside him, awakened by her affection, and he fell for it. But he didn't feel betrayed. A sense of failure consumed him instead. He proved incapable of earning the status conferred by her approval, and a spacious absence resounded in his interior. The role he wore around it had been destroyed, and now Tomiina was trying to destroy its fleshy enclosure.

Lionel worried about being stuck at the Hotel Bellehaven forever, but now that he was leaving, it was almost nostalgic. He befriended none of his coworkers. What were their names? Some impermeable membrane prevented him from becoming their companions and sealed off unknown potentials that he might have explored if he stayed. Would they even notice he was gone? He had been more of a guest than an employee after all, in spite of Damian's objections.

Doing a final pass through the house, Lionel came upon the dashiki that Tony gave him. He climbed into it and left without shutting the door.

Lionel pulled up to Tony's house as the sun finished setting. There was no answer when he pushed the call button at the gate, so he started honking his horn. After a long pause, the gate parted at the center, and he sped up the driveway.

Tony emerged from the front entrance in a silk robe. He stopped on the stone landing with his hands on his hips, resembling a concerned father whose teenager came home past curfew. Lionel got out of his car and stumbled to the steps beneath the landing. He looked up at Tony, then adjusted his dashiki.

"They're trying to kill me."

"Who?" Tony scanned the perimeter of his lawn.

"They want to sacrifice me in a religious ritual."

"So you led them here?"

Lionel shrugged. With a flat face, Tony ushered him inside, looking over his shoulder before shutting and locking the door.

In a sitting room near the entrance, Tony sat in an ornate armchair while Lionel peeked out the window between the drapes. A white marble coffee table served as the centerpiece of the room under a crystal chandelier, and a white Persian rug with blue floral patterns lay beneath.

From an ivory jewelry box on the table next to him, Tony withdrew a bundle of sage and lit its jagged stems. As he shook out the flame and blew into the embers, a thin line of fragrant smoke rose from the bundle and wafted toward Lionel. Tony crossed to him and began adorning him with its cool scent.

Lionel knocked the bundle out of his hand.

"Dude." Tony crouched to pick it up. "That's a Nain rug. Four layers in the warp thread."

"I'm losing it." Lionel sat in the chair opposite Tony's, his reflection distorting in a silver champagne ice bucket on the coffee table. He picked it up and pressed his forehead against the condensation.

"Can I offer you a joint?"

"Oh, thank god."

Tony touched his hand to the ivory jewelry box, but he paused, inspired. "Matter fact, you want to hit The Exorcist?"

"What's The Exorcist?"

The Exorcist was a large, multi-chamber glass marijuana smoking system that took up most of the coffee table. Its intricate network of tubes, recyclers, and honeycomb percolators improved on the traditional bong's design and water filtration, delivering a hit of flower, wax, and vaporized THC simultaneously. Tony had Marcus bring it down and prepare the exorcism.

The built-in torch for the dab rig, the vaporizer plate, and the smoke-flow regulator hydraulic pump required it to be plugged into the wall. Ground flower went into the vape chamber and the dark blue bowl resting on a glass stem protruding from the top. Marcus dabbed wax into an opening on the end of a compartment that swung out on a hinge.

"Press the white button when you're ready." Marcus readied his lighter.

Lionel got down on his knees and put his lips to the mouthpiece. Without further reflection, he pressed the white button. Marcus lit the dark blue bowl, and the built-in torch flared into the wax compartment with the sound of surging pressurized air. The vape chamber glowed red with a small LED light bulb (purely for aesthetic effect) as Lionel inhaled through the mouthpiece.

Milk-white smoke from the bowl and dab rig bubbled through the serpentine maze of glass. The cyclone chamber's coil mixed the smoke with the vapor, and the hydraulic pump blew the mix gently into Lionel's tar-encrusted lungs. Tony grinned, impressed at the fortitude with which Lionel inhaled.

Lionel shrugged and said "That—" but just what that referred to never made it out. A coughing fit came upon him, and he tried to exhale all the smoke, but it clenched his inflamed, trembling lungs in a hot iron grip.

"There it is," said Tony, laughing.

Lionel's eyes watered as a cataclysmic high permeated every cell of his body, even aching in his teeth. Marcus helped him into an armchair and offered a hit to Tony.

"Nah. The Exorcist is a little too much."

The lights in the room glowed brighter for Lionel as though they were diffused through clouds. His brain shook a small sound into his ears when he closed his eyes. Tony lit a joint and sat back in his chair, nodding to Marcus, who unplugged The Exorcist and carried it out of the room. Reflexive trembling started in Lionel's abdomen, and try as he might to rest against the chair, tension lifted his hips up and out a few inches like he was trying to levitate.

"This wouldn't have anything to do with Adhikashara, would it?" Tony's words sang with transcendent portent made graver by his nonchalance as if he were unaware that divinity shone through him. "Is that why they're coming to kill you?"

"I don't know," Lionel managed to say with labored speech. Tony seemed to be leaning away from him ever so slightly, politely not mentioning whatever Lionel was doing with his face. "I was being deposed for... I don't know why."

"Been there."

"And I thought—"

A flapping sound occurred behind Lionel, and a teal blur shot over his head. He dove to the ground and covered the back of his neck, and his heart pounded like it had every intention of breaking through his ribcage. The blue floral pattern on the rug squirmed in Lionel's vision. Peeking up to see if anyone was trying to kill him, he saw a teal macaw perched on Tony's forearm.

"I've gotten so used to Dave, I forgot people are afraid of birds." Tony petted Dave's feathers lovingly. "He was a gift from Ron Jeremy."

Lionel collected himself and climbed back into the armchair across from Tony's. Movement appeared in Lionel's periphery and he flinched away from it. It was his own reflection in the champagne ice bucket that Marcus moved onto an end table.

"So the deposition..."

"My boss wants to kill me. And maybe Tomiina too."

"Okay, start with the boss. Is he suing you?"

"No. I don't know. He said when I dropped the boxes off here, after actually, and before I came back to get them... he said he was going to tear my teeth out."

"That's specific. But that wouldn't kill you. It wouldn't feel good though. Did he say he was going to kill you?"

"No."

"See, unless someone tells you to your face they're going to kill you, they won't do shit. He probably just said that as an expression."

Lionel shook his head side to side with his eyes closed in an emphatic no, catalyzing a falling sensation which he tried to offset by rising in his chair. The acrid taste of smoke lingered in his raw, dry mouth. Halfway through an attempt to swallow, he panicked that his throat was stuck and that he would suffocate. He gasped for air at last.

"I found teeth at the hotel."

"After he told you that?"

"Before."

Tony considered for a moment with pursed lips. Turning to Dave, he said, "That is concerning for sure. But what does that have to do with the deposition?"

"The lawyer. She was all bandaged up and her face was swollen."

"Car accident?"

"No. She asked if I tried to sacrifice her in a religious ritual."

"Did you?"

"I'm an atheist."

"But did you try to—"

"No!"

"All right." Tony held up his Dave-free hand up innocently. "I'm just trying to get up to speed. Did she have all her teeth?"

"Yeah, but at the deposition, she said Tomiina is working against me."

Tony opened his mouth, squinting. He began to object but decided against it. Dave nibbled one of his dreadlocks.

"Tomiina? She black?"

"White. This girl I was involved with. Tomiina Deatherage. She's famous."

"Oh shit, that girl from *Night in Shining Armoire?* You know, I thought it was a little cheesy, but it had a lot of heart. Wait. You're dating her? Lionel!"

"Not exactly."

"But the lawyer who's all beat up said she's trying to kill you?"

"I don't know if she's trying to kill me. But she might be working against me. And it turns out that she might be working with her father."

"Hold up. One thing at a time. You said she's working against you. What exactly is she doing?"

"Melanie Bobbers said—"

"Wait. Who is Melanie Bobbers?"

"The lawyer from the deposition."

"The one with the bandages?"

"Yes. She said that Tomiina is trying to... She actually implied that she might have an ulterior motive."

"Okay..."

"Also her dad worked with my grandpa."

"Melanie's dad?"

"Tomiina's dad."

"Ah. Not exactly damning."

"At the hotel!"

"This famous girl's dad works at a hotel? You'd think she'd help him out."

"They're on the board. Her dad and my grandpa." Lionel stared at Tony, waiting for the gravity of the situation to hit him. Tony stroked his chin.

"Ay, Marcus. Bring some shrimp in here. Also, it's time for Dave's exercises."

Marcus entered the sitting room to retrieve Dave, and Dave flapped his wings as Tony handed him off without looking at Marcus. The appearance of the room lifted from its fixity and translated itself into legible signs rising out of the rote shapes in Lionel's perception, and he held onto the arms of the chair, leaving handprints of sweat beneath his grip.

"It'll be about ten minutes on the shrimp," said Marcus.

Tony groaned. "Do you like shrimp?"

"Sure." Lionel was barely aware of what he agreed to.

"Ay, Marcus. Bring some for Lionel too." Tony rose from the chair and stretched, starting to walk out of the room. He paused and sat back down. "So this girl's dad, the hotel. Go on."

"And my grandpa."

"What's he got to do with this?"

"He got me the job."

"Where?"

"At the hotel."

"You work there too?"

"Yes!"

"You never told me that." Tony relit his joint and looked away. Suddenly, he sat up in his chair. "Your boss! He knows this girl's dad and your grandpa. I get it. And all that came up in the deposition?"

"Yes. The deposition was for the lawsuit I got from my grandpa. They're all in the foundation I'm the president of."

"And you didn't know they knew each other?"

"I didn't even know I was the president."

"So just ask your grandpa about it."

"He's dead."

Tony nodded. He sat back, and treading lightly, he asked, "Was he sacrificed in a religious ritual?"

"Not that I know of."

"All right. So all these people know each other..."

"Yeah."

"So what?"

"And the lawyer almost got sacrificed."

"Were they the ones who did it?"

"She thought it was me, which makes me think it was them."

"What did she say exactly?"

"You kinda had to be there. In context, she was talking about them and the sacrifice."

"And now you think they're trying to do that to you?"

"They are, Tony. I can't prove it. I just know."

Tony sucked air through his teeth. He got on his feet and crossed to the champagne ice bucket. After futzing with the foil on the top, he popped the cork out and took a swig. "You want some?" Lionel nodded. "Ay Marcus! Bring Lionel some champagne! And have Tiff make us some cookies!" Tony returned to his chair. "Here's the thing, Lionel. This is definitely strange. And the lawyer being all beat up is no joke."

"And the teeth."

"Yeah, that's some scary shit. But... like, where's the smoking gun?"

"Huh?"

"This is all a lot of he-said-she-said and what-have-yous, but how do you know they want to kill you?"

Lionel pondered for a moment. "I know it's not logical... Melanie said they'll try to get rid of me."

"How does she know?"

"I don't know. But they tried to do it to her."

"Go back to your girlfriend. What's up with her?"

"We got into an argument recently."

"About what?"

"It was—well, I accidentally said we were dating, and she did not like that." Tony winced, and Lionel nodded with his eyes half-closed. "I actually said 'involved,' but she kissed me earlier that night, so... I don't know. She drove me crazy. But she was the only thing in my life that made me feel good."

Tony smiled sadly. He touched a picture frame on the end table next to his chair. "I once had a love like that."

"Is that her?"

"This? No, this is a production assistant I worked with. Odd present. And it was *her* birthday. No. Before I entered the industry, I worked in a coffee shop, and one day, in walked Sylvia. It was like... you know when a shooting star crosses the sky?"

"I'm not in the mood."

"Perhaps another time," said Tony wistfully, stamping out his joint in an ashtray. "How'd she drive you crazy?"

"She was so irrational. All women are like that."

Tony considered for a moment. "This line producer I work with is pretty rational. She's like a goddamn robot."

Lionel stewed. "She was manipulating me the whole time. She never would have been with..." Lionel gestured to himself. "It was all a part of the plan."

"But, Lionel. How do you know?"

"I just know."

"Did you call the police?"

"They're probably in with the police!"

"Lionel, bud. This is a little... Do you know for sure?"

"I don't have anything else to go on."

Marcus entered with two plates with shrimp arranged in a circle around a metal cup of cocktail sauce. Tony clapped his hands together and sat up. He pinched a piece of shrimp off the plate before Marcus finished setting it on the table. Lionel stared at his plate with no appetite, but he ate a single piece to be polite.

With his mouth full, Tony said, "If there's this conspiracy to kill her—"

"To kill *me*."

"To kill anybody. Why didn't they do it already? You've been running around with that girl and working with everybody, so why'd they wait so long?"

Lionel wasn't paying attention. The elevated significance of the shifting surfaces in his vision intermingled with his racing thoughts, and the two became indistinguishable.

"They're all working together. It's like they've got this cabal."

"Cabal?" Tony furrowed his brow. "They Jewish?"

"Huh?"

"This Jewish actress and her dad are conspiring to do a ritual sacrifice? Are you aware that that is an antisemitic trope?"

"I don't know if they're Jewish."

"Do you think they control the banks and the media too?"

"No, they're controlling me!"

"Did you know antisemitic hate crimes have been on the rise?"

"Is Deatherage a Jewish name?"

"They could have changed it. Happens a lot. Look it up."

"I don't care why they're trying to kill me. I didn't even know they were Jewish. Also, accusing someone of being hateful usually just means you don't have an argument."

"Argument?" Tony was more confused at this than anything else Lionel said thus far. "I'm trying to help you, little boy." He shook his head and turned his attention to his shrimp. They were both silent as he finished his plate and licked his fingers clean. The smell of cookies in the oven entered the room.

Lionel closed his eyes and rested his head on the back of his chair. Shivers passed through him, and he tried to breathe calmly to stop them. Marcus entered with a champagne ice bucket for Lionel and set it on the coffee table. Tony rearranged his dreadlocks and sat back, crossing his legs.

"So what do you want?"

Lionel hadn't thought of that. "I just had to get out of there. I didn't have anywhere else to go."

"You can crash if you need to. I'm not really seeing any imminent danger." Tony's eyes flickered to the window. Standing, he said, "But it seems appropriate to me, Lionel, that we do some sort of exchange. Maybe you coming here tonight was a synchronicity." Lionel groaned and threw himself against the back of his chair. "Okay, I'm going to lay it out. You can stay here as long as you want if you can get me Adhikashara."

"I don't know where to get it."

"I do. I found directions in the documents you brought here."

"Why didn't you go get it?"

"I can't just show up asking for drugs. But you could. They're yours."

"I sold a little weed. But this seems more serious."

"Think of the potential, Lionel. With that drug, you won't need what's her face anymore. You could ascend to another plane."

"I'm already having a hard time with this one."

"You don't have to do it. Just sell some to me. Matter fact, let's trade. Adhikashara for an unlimited stay here. Actually, a one-month stay."

Lionel pondered. "I really don't think—" Tiffany, six feet tall and naked beneath her apron, entered the room with a plate of cookies. She set the cookies down and exited. "I'm in. But could we do three months? It's going to be hard to get a job with the economy and all that."

"Deal. But I want to see you sending out applications."

It wasn't until after Tony set him up in a guest bedroom with a king-size canopy bed and a full bathroom with a Jacuzzi next to a balcony that overlooked the tennis court in the backyard that it occurred to Lionel that he was unemployed and homeless. Maybe this mystery drug of his grandfather's could create some cash flow. But how long would it last? What price would it fetch? Lionel could always upcharge his potential buyers as he did in college when someone would slip in for an eighth and concoct flimsy excuses for why they couldn't stay and smoke with him.

Unless he could provide something, everyone hurried to leave him. Damian used him for his labor, however pitiful and unproductive. His grandfather and father used him to pass off their problems and wash their hands. And now Tony was using him for drugs. But Tomiina, what did she want from him? He never offered her anything. Even when he believed her affections, he was suspicious that she was not attracted to him. So what was it? And his mother, what had he given her? Maybe the absence of anything to offer, either tangible or inside of himself, sent both of them for the door. Accompanying his fear for his life and the throb in his head from his diminishing high was the incongruous feeling that he somehow let his mother down and that all her pain, pain he could never understand, was his fault.

He climbed into the canopy bed and cried into its silk sheets.

Chapter 16

An inconspicuous gathering of Joshua trees almost entirely obscured a gravel road that departed from the highway. The road stretched far into the distance where there were no human structures within eyeshot and descended out of view into a valley. Tony winced as his white Rolls Royce, which collected a layer of gravel dust, drove over potholes and bumps. In the passenger seat, Lionel rocked back and forth with the bumpy ride and the nervous dancing of his insides, which had kept him up most of the night.

The surfaces of the objects in the guest room moved about in the dark, taunting him by returning to their inert position the moment he looked at them directly. He was disappointed in his inability to enjoy the amenities in his new room. The space around him sealed itself off as though forbidding him from occupying it.

Overhead, a red-tailed hawk glided lazily, surveying the barren landscape. They reached a locked farm gate that blocked the road, and Tony slowed to a stop in front of it. They shared a look.

"I guess we can't go any farther," said Lionel. "At least we tried."

"Nah, we'll figure something out. We're talking about the source of power over everything. I'm not turning back."

Tony got out of the car and looked into the distance, using his hand as a visor. There was no wind to offset the heat of the sun that had him sweating through his purple Rocawear track jacket the moment he stepped out of the car. Desert agave, yucca, and cacti reached their violent points all around him, protecting their pulpy insides, and the loose soil in the spaces around them was dry and dead.

Tony returned to the car and held his hand against the AC vent.

"There's someone coming," said Lionel, peering out the window.

In the distance, a figure approached. Waves of heat danced around it, interplaying its edges with the background. They watched silently as it emerged—it was a man in a bucket hat, Oakley sunglasses, and a Hawaiian shirt. It was not until he arrived at Tony's car that they noticed an assault rifle slung over his shoulder.

Lionel looked to Tony for reassurance, which he met with a pacifying hand. Tony lowered the passenger window, and Lionel sank down with it.

"Y'all here for a geodesic dome?" said the man.

Tony looked to Lionel and then back to the man.

"Yes," said Tony as Lionel simultaneously said "No."

"We're mostly just shopping around at this juncture," said Tony.

The man opened the farm gate and waved them in while saying something into a walkie-talkie clipped to his Hawaiian shirt.

Beyond the gate, the stretch of road descended into a valley. Rounding the corner, they drove into what looked like a construction site. Geodesic domes that resembled igloos stood in various stages of completion. The domes were made of beams arranged in triangles that were bolted together into polyhedrons. Some rested on foundations of stacked tires packed with concrete. In a clearing beyond the perimeter of the lot sat a helicopter on its pad.

Men dressed like the gate attendant stomped around the perimeter of the lot, stacked sandbags, and lazily rested their hands on their assault rifles. The air smelled like gunpowder.

"Turn around," said Lionel. "They probably knew I'd go here, and they're—oh god. They're going to execute us."

"Lionel, chill," said Tony. "When you sell drugs, it's smart to have a little protection. They just happen to have an armed militia."

They rolled to a stop near a row of dirt bikes, and a boy of about eighteen came up to their car. The sides of his head were shaved, and he had long hair on top.

"Hiya," said the boy with a big smile that bulged the pouch of dip in his bottom lip. His canine teeth grew out of his gums in front of the rest of his teeth. "What can I do ya for?"

Tony gestured that he was going to exit the car, and the boy gave him the go-ahead. As they spoke, Lionel sat stiffly, fearing that any movement would provoke a barrage of bullets. Gunshots sounded from across the lot, and he cried out. In the distance, a group of men ran tactical drills, falling to the ground, training their scopes on bales of hay, and firing.

With heavy breath, Lionel shot his eyes to Tony who had his hands on the car. The boy was patting him down. Tony glared through the window as though this had been Lionel's idea.

"Simple precaution, sir," said the boy. He tapped on the windshield. "You're next, buddy."

Lionel got out of the car slowly, trembling. The boy gave him a quick pat-down and said into his walkie-talkie, "All clear."

Tony's shoulders were hunched. Twice, he checked behind him to make sure no one was sneaking up on them. The only person behind him was Lionel, hiding like a child behind a parent. On one of Tony's uncertain looks over his shoulder, Lionel thought he saw the same look of disapproval and disgust that Damian showed him when he did just about anything at all.

The boy beckoned them to a cluster of domes on display with little flower gardens in front of them and welcome mats at their entrances. One of them had a wooden plank attached to a support beam that read in flamboyant hand-drawn font, "God Bless This Mess."

"My name is Caleb, and I'll be helping you." His smile showed off his fangs. "We build our domes out of triangles for the most efficient weight distribution. The triangles are also a nod to Pythagoras, one of the pillars of Western civilization."

"That checks out," said Lionel, still afraid.

"They make for quick assembly and disassembly if you ever need to get up and go on short notice. They load easy into a flatbed. We've got gun rack attachments, chimney options, domes for kids. Introduce 'em early. My wife and I got one for our youngest son." Caleb pointed to a small boy running drills, strapped with an assault rifle like the rest. "How can I assist you today?" Caleb turned to them with a toothy grin.

"What do you use these for?" said Tony.

"Private security. The only legitimate form of security, I might add. A government monopoly on security is a threat to everyone's safety and to our second amendment rights, which we're pretty big fans of around here."

"Anyone come for the guns yet?" said Tony.

"Little by little. Not here, but they're trying all the time. Our measures are preventative, but we're keeping sharp too for the Boo–," his smile faltered. "For the future. When we rebuild, after the federal government falls of course, an armed militia with geodesic domes is just about all you need. Can I interest you in a dome today?"

"How do y'all feel about black people?" said Tony.

"Shoot, we've got a few in our ranks," said Caleb, looking out over the training ground, blocking the sun from his eyes. "He must have wandered off somewhere. But unless someone's taking our guns or damaging our property, we don't have problems with anyone. Provided they abide by the non-aggression principle, naturally."

Tony took off his sunglasses and brushed his dreads behind his shoulders.

"You've been great, Caleb," said Tony. "But we were hoping to speak to the manager... or foreman... commander? We've got a special request."

"I handle the custom domes, sir. We can even do a presidential hall of fame like Epcot, but it'll cost ya," said Caleb with customer service panache.

"We were hoping to procure," said Tony, lowering his voice, "Adhikashara."

This knocked the friendly yokel right out of Caleb. Silence hung over their group for a moment. He narrowed his eyes and adjusted the assault rifle on his shoulder.

"Come again?" said Caleb.

"Adhikashara?" said Tony.

Caleb stepped back slowly with his eyes trained on them. Speaking into his walkie-talkie, he said, "We've got a situation."

"We don't mean any harm, sir," said Tony. "Matter fact, we were just about to head out." Tony took a step toward their car.

"Hold it right there," said Caleb. "I'm gonna need you to stay right where you are." Keeping his eyes on them, Caleb approached a large, canvas-covered dome. The moment he slipped inside, Tony and Lionel started bickering in lowered voices. The other men noticed them and squared up to the scene.

"They're gonna kill us."

"They're gonna kill me."

"He said they're cool with black people."

"You believe him?"

"I didn't want to come here."

"We're here now."

Caleb opened the flaps and beckoned them inside. Tony entered slowly, Lionel hiding behind him. A savory smell met them there. There was a catering table with stainless steel chafer dishes and trays holding mounds of mashed potatoes, pot roast, and brisket.

At the back of the dome sat a sweaty, shirtless man, fanning himself with a newspaper. Armed guards stood on either side of him.

Tony adjusted his stance and met the gaze of the man seated.

"We mean no harm, sir," said Tony. "We just wanted to pick up."

Lionel let out a little whimper.

"Caleb said you were speaking Arabic," said the man. "These guys don't look Middle Eastern."

Lionel recognized his voice.

"Adhikashara," said Tony. "We were hoping to procure my boss's product. Then we'll be on our way."

"Is that anything like Allahu Akbar?" said Caleb.

"Dad?" said Lionel, creeping out from behind Tony. Francis was startled to see him. The two looked at each other for a while without speaking, and the guards exchanged glances.

In spite of everything Lionel feared would come to pass, his mind was free of resentment. He tried to decide just what his father's presence indicated, but nothing came to him. His eyes finally adjusted to the dim light inside, and he became hopeful that his father would feed him.

"Have you been here the whole time?" said Lionel.

"It wasn't safe for me anymore," said Francis. "I'm glad you're okay."

"My boss and a movie star are trying to kill me."

"You can stay here, Lionel. It's safe. "

"Did you have anything to do with this?"

"With what?"

"Oh, you know... Melanie Bobbers said that Tomiina is trying to... or that it's kind of strange that a celebrity would... Are you trying to kill me?"

"Of course not. I've been here. I didn't want you to fend for yourself, but I had no choice. I planned to send for you once I was sure that it was safe here. But you made it here on your own. You must have a lot of questions. If you stay, we can straighten it all out. I'll tell you everything."

"I'm actually living at Tony's now. He's got a kick-ass house. And AC."

"Staying," said Tony, "until you can get back on your feet."

"Who knows how long that'll take," said Lionel, pulling up his pants which had ridden low down his butt. "We came for Adhikashara. Is it here?"

"I would advise against it."

"I don't want any," said Lionel. "Tony's the one who's all excited about it."

"It's very powerful. It's best not to tamper with your mind that way."

"Have you tried it?"

"I have. It destroyed everything for me for a while."

"What happened?" said Lionel.

Francis considered for a moment.

"In order for it to show what holds the ultimate power in your life, it breaks everything down. Your sense of self, the thoughts in your head, your entire ability to construct meaning. It shows you that you are nothing. And for me... it showed me that the ultimate power in my life was my proclivity to break everything down, a habit I got from my father. I had an answer for everything, and I could spin a web around anyone who objected to me.

"It worked on everyone. I could prove how whatever anyone said was false, a power play, a feeble attempt to best me. It worked on your mother until she stopped caring about being right. She just wanted to get rid of me, and with your grandpa... It was impossible for us to communicate at the end. I tried to show him his errors, but past a certain age, it's useless to try to change someone.

"I saw that I was so good at tearing down, I didn't know how to build. Adhikashara shattered everything for me. An infinite void is the only thing that was left. And I tried to argue that away too. But I had nothing. I became nothing. So throwing nothing into nothing doesn't destroy the nothingness, it's just nothing. It's zero plus zero. Don't go near it. It's better to have the courage to believe in something. It doesn't have to be perfect, but it builds a safe haven against chaos. You can't build a foundation on nihilism. That's why I came here. We're building a future that can withstand the test of time. Entropy will erode anything that doesn't fortify itself with strong principles."

"Entropy?" said Lionel.

"That and the liberal media. Universities are guilty too. And they say it's progress," said Francis, making air quotes around progress. "But it's simply the decay of traditional institutions. It's pretty convenient to claim a natural process like entropic decay as a political stance. Not to mention shortsighted. That's like advocating for the sun to come out tomorrow, and feeling responsible and accomplished at sunrise. It's a self-important, mindless ideology."

"Yeah, but if it's inevitable," said Tony, "doesn't that mean progressives are on the right side of history?"

Francis smiled. "They are until it all collapses. From a bird's eye view of history, the fall of institutions is a victory until there are no institutions left. But I agree. It is inevitable. Progressives are better gamblers. I'm not a conservative. Conservatives are trying to drag us back to a time that's dead and gone. It was dead and gone even when it was here. We have our minds on the future. We want to usher in a new society post-collapse. One that will last. We'll build something worth conserving. And we'll urge the collapse in the meantime."

Tony was lost in thought over Francis's words. Lionel's pinky was knuckle-deep in his left ear, twisting toward an itch that was just out of reach.

"Is Adhikashara here or not?" said Lionel.

Francis sighed. "Did you listen to a word I just said?"

"Entropy is bad, and the liberal media has an agenda," said Lionel. "I agree. We're here for Adhikashara."

"It isn't here," said Francis, massaging his temple.

"Do you know where we can get it? We drove all the way out here."

"I beg you to stay. This is the last safe place for me. If you leave, I'll consider this meeting a threat to our security, which is the most important thing of all."

"Along with private property rights," Caleb chimed in.

"I won't tell anyone," said Lionel.

"That doesn't matter. We'll move to a new location that cannot be found. The domes make for quick disassembly. You can load them right into a flatbed."

"It's too hot," said Lionel.

"Panic attack?" asked Tony.

"Nah. Just kinda sweaty," said Lionel. "I couldn't live like this. No offense. I'm a little scared of guns too, to be honest."

"I understand. That's your decision. In that case, I'll ask you to leave. Caleb will take you back to your car."

Caleb approached them with a tablet and had them put in their emails. He gave his rehearsed spiel. "You can opt out at any time. Please be on the lookout for our fall sale. It's a 20% off blowout where we flip all inventory, and on the last day it's 35% off. You'll also be automatically enrolled in a raffle for a set of targets, cookware, and a free day of training for your militia. Here is our complimentary tote bag."

Caleb led them back to the car. He gave them a wave and said, "I'm sorry about the misunderstanding."

They drove out of the lot in silence. Once the gate attendant let them leave, Lionel peered into his tote bag. Inside was a brochure, a copy of *Atlas Shrugged*, and a bottle of supplements called Right Brain. Tony's eye's flickered toward him occasionally, but Lionel looked out the window.

"So are we going to talk about the right-wing militia? Or are you just gonna pretend that didn't happen?"

"I didn't know anything about this," said Lionel. "You were the one who drove us to a bunker with a bunch of machine guns."

"Do you think I liked being the only black guy walking into all those white supremacists?

"White supremacists? Where did you get that?" said Lionel. "It seemed like they were into freedom. And the West, probably. "

"Oh yeah, never heard that one before," said Tony with a flat face. "What about you? Are you into the West?"

Smelling a trick question, Lionel said, "No."

"All right," said Tony, but he still seemed suspicious. Leaning to the side, he withdrew a folded piece of paper from his back pocket. "We checked that off the list. Now I know for sure where it is. It's at a house down in Palos Verdes."

Lionel gaped at Tony.

"What's the address?" said Lionel. Tony showed it to him. "That's my grandpa's house."

"Interesting."

"It's not interesting," said Lionel. "What if they try to kill me there?"

"Isn't your grandpa dead?"

"His maid still lives there," said Lionel. "Maybe he put in his will 'murder my grandson if he stops by.'"

"Lionel," said Tony, lifting his track jacket to reveal something tucked in his waistband. "We good."

"A gun?"

"Pepper spray."

"Like that'll work."

"I also trained in Krav Maga for a film," said Tony. "*Jabs of Submission.* Ever seen it?"

"Why didn't we go there first?" said Lionel, pouting out the window.

"I didn't know whose house it was. There were a lot of papers in those boxes. I made a guess, and I was wrong. And excuse me for wanting to see some goddamn Joshua trees."

"We could have avoided that whole ordeal."

"I had a choice between a residential address in a city full of retired Republicans and an encampment in the middle of the desert. Where would you look for a bunch of psychedelic drugs?"

"You're an idiot."

"You're a racist."

"Oh here we go! That's what everyone says when you disagree. Why don't you engage with my argument?"

"What's your argument?"

"I mean... like... in general..."

"That's what I thought."

They rode in silence for more than an hour, the afternoon sun glaring in their faces. They passed billboards for gas stations with buffets and resort oases, and signs of civilization became more frequent. The density of traffic increased in Palm Springs, and the surrounding mountains trapped dry heat. A car tailed them as they entered the corridor of mall complexes and car dealerships beside the freeways that fed back into Los Angeles.

A red-tailed hawk glided in wide arcs above their car.

"Do you ever wish you could fly?" said Lionel, staring out the window.

"You can," said Tony. "Just go to LAX."

"It would be nice to have that view over everything all the time."

"Nah," said Tony. "You can't see people from up there."

Chapter 17

Lionel and Tony sat in Art's living room as she bustled about, cleaning every surface in sight. Even Lionel's shoulders got a quick wipe where dandruff accumulated. Constance greeted them at the door holding a rag and an aerosol dust cleaner. Her dark eyes looked heavier than when Lionel had seen her last. The walls were barren except for holes from hanging pictures that were sold in the estate sale.

At last, Constance started to sit, but before her butt hit the chair, the oven timer beeped. She excused herself, smiling.

After their arrival, Tony had walked to the edge of the cliffs for pictures. Lionel was his unwilling photographer, holding Tony's phone lazily with no attention to composition. As Tony scrolled through his pictures shaking his head, Constance returned with a pile of palmier pastries and set them on the coffee table. She rested in the recliner opposite them, her hands comforting each other.

"You look well, Lionel," said Constance. "How is your friend?"

"Why don't you ask him?"

"I'm good," said Tony with a mouthful of palmier. He wiped his mouth with the back of his hand. "You have a lovely home."

"Thank you," said Constance. "But I mean your girlfriend."

"Oh," said Lionel. "We're on a bit of a break."

"I'm sorry," said Constance, sad for him, which made him feel that he had made her sad.

"It's for the best," said Lionel. "It was mutual."

"I thought y'all weren't dating?" said Tony.

"That's neither here nor there," said Lionel, pretending to be distracted with palmier crumbs on his shirt. "But it turned out she wasn't exactly who she said she was. Actually, it's much worse than that. She was actively trying to destroy me."

Constance touched her hand to her jaw. "Sometimes when we're angry, we ascribe motives to others."

"I'm not angry," said Lionel. "I received some information, and the whole thing seems pretty clear. She was trying to use her feminine mystery powers to butter me up for something."

"For what?" said Constance.

"I don't know," said Lionel, eyeing her. "Something to do with the foundation. By the way, I probably should have asked this by now, but what is the foundation exactly? The Fiduciary Realities thing?"

"Royalties," said Constance, adjusting her apron. After a moment of deliberation, she said, "It's registered as a charitable foundation. 501(c)(3). Tax-exempt. They used it to launder money."

Lionel nodded, but he was dissatisfied. How much did Constance know? She could be lying to obscure the foundation's murderous intentions. Her demure hospitality and unassuming smile could all be an act. He helped himself to another palmier.

"I thought they were trying to...," said Lionel, but he stopped. "To be fair, I actually don't know what it was. But I was wrong, I guess."

"I hope you don't think I had anything to do with it," said Constance, as though she read his mind. She had simply read his face. "Art blamed me for his legal troubles and I nev–," her voice broke, "I never learned what he thought I did. So if you've come down to accuse me further, I think it's best you leave. I can hardly bear it." She cried openly.

Tony rose and put a hand on her back.

"He didn't mean it, ma'am," said Tony. "He's just a little shaken up. We've had a long day with white supremacists. And he's got some lady problems he's workin' through." Tony silently motioned for Lionel to say something.

"Sorry," said Lionel in a hollow tone.

Constance excused herself into the master bedroom.

"That poor woman is crying."

"She was with my grandpa," said Lionel loudly, and Tony hushed him. Whispering, Lionel said, "She told me they used to fuck all around the house. We don't know if she's in on all this or not. She could be faking it."

"You are out of your mind," said Tony.

"You entered the picture like a second ago," said Lionel. "You don't know what's going on."

"Neither do you," said Tony. "You didn't say shit about money laundering. What if that's all it is?"

Lionel paused to consider. Had he made too many assumptions? He had no way of knowing if Melanie made up everything about the sacrificial ritual. She could have faked her injuries to play the victim. As much as he hated to admit being wrong, it would come as a huge relief if this whole conspiracy were revealed to be nothing more than a corporate tax dodge.

"That's still bad." Lionel began to hyperventilate. "I could go to prison."

"Better alive in prison than dead."

"Is it?"

"Fair point."

Tony left the living room, and a dissociative lapse was coming upon Lionel. He closed his eyes and slowed his breathing. There was a small knock on the door of the master bedroom, and Constance let Tony in and closed the door behind them.

Lionel opened his eyes to remind himself of the stability of the world, naming the objects in front of him and trying to focus on their harmlessness.

Beneath his controlled calm swirled a continuum of thoughts and perceptions and even feelings, such as the sensation that his disintegrated essence extended into the room around him, maybe farther than that, in spite of his best efforts to know himself as a discrete object. These efforts never worked. Nonetheless, he stuck to his story that he was his genes, his neurons firing off, and his pitiful body, nothing else.

Lionel's being might as well have been modeled on the Fiduciary Royalties Association for United Donors. After all, he was a stand-in for a capable person, lazy consciousness deposited into a body that didn't want to expend energy that benefited society. The little effort he put into his life involved consuming things that made rich men richer. Melanie seemed to think he owed debts to the world, and it seemed there was something mysterious going on inside him. He might have settled the matter by registering himself as a 501(c)(3) organization.

This was no different than the notion that he was his body, an identity he wore like an ill-fitting costume, measured with height and weight percentiles relative to others in his demographic. It was just another placeholder, a hollow description that shirked its responsibility, avoiding the hard work of defining him.

Who would have believed him if he said how he really felt? Putting it into words produced intolerable nonsense: "I feel like I'm watching myself fulfill my inevitable path that was laid out before my birth. I recognize myself in other people's eyes. Animals have personalities. The letters in words look like people flexing their arms. My interior just fell down even though my body didn't move. I feel like I'm hanging off the top of my head and a few feet in front of it. When I'm about to fall asleep, all of my thoughts blur together and become symmetrical reflections of each other. I feel like a 501(c)(3) organization."

Lionel dismissed it all as random combinations of irrational thoughts, but it all leaked out slowly and persistently as a feeling.

Being seated on the couch prevented the lapse from boiling over into an existentially threatening nightmare as it usually did. The solitude helped as well. Perhaps he was getting used to them. He breathed through it, and it began to subside. By the time Tony and Constance returned, he was munching on a palmier, content.

"You're ready to ascend?" said Constance, wiping away her tears.

"Huh?"

"I can guide you, Lionel," said Constance. "It would be my honor."

"I'm not sure I follow."

"Adhikashara," said Tony, grinning.

"We were just hoping to pick up," said Lionel. "I don't want to take it."

"It would be irresponsible to give it to you if you have not taken it first. The mother is very powerful. You cannot show her to other people without meeting her yourself."

Tony nodded, his eyes wide with excitement.

"I'm more of a weed guy," said Lionel.

"She wants to meet you. It's her will," said Constance. "She carries the whole universe in her womb. You already know her, but you've forgotten."

"Who are you talking about?"

"It will all become clear," said Constance with a knowing smile. She went into the kitchen, and Lionel craned his head to see what she was doing.

"I didn't sign up for this," said Lionel.

"We drove all the way down here," said Tony, his face stern. "We are not leaving empty-handed."

"I want no part in this." Lowering his voice, Lionel said, "What was that shit about the universe?"

"Lionel, we are taking that mysterious drug."

"I'm not." Lionel crossed his arms. "You go ahead."

"Fine. You can find your own place to live. But you'll have to wait till tomorrow. I'm taking it with or without you."

It crossed Lionel's mind that he could live with Constance, but he immediately dismissed the idea. He was still not convinced that she was uninvolved with the foundation nor that the impending religious sacrifice was only a delusion. He chewed his lip.

"We're on cliffs above the beach with a beautiful woman cooking us drugs," said Tony. "We're doing it."

Chapter 18

Lionel sipped the brew, and its bitterness hit sharply at the back of his tongue. It had a chemical taste similar to how paint smells. He forced himself to swallow it. He and Tony were seated on mats in the backyard. Constance presided from the porch, ladling Adhikashara from a pot. Rustling in the bushes sounded, but it was too dark out to see anything.

Lionel sat back on his mat. The brew digesting in his gut induced an internal emptiness, a dreadful sinking sensation that intensified until it vibrated through him and all of his muscles came alive with it. The brain fog that kept him down and dim cleared like smoke in the wind.

He peered at Constance who sat on the porch enjoying the night air as though she were willfully ignoring the imminent danger and fear he felt. Tony lay next to him with his eyes closed and an open-mouthed smile on his face.

Vast openness awakened in Lionel's interior, and his sense of self had way more room to stretch its legs. It drifted just to the left of his skull, where he observed the aggregate of sensations formerly known as Lionel carry on believing it was in charge. Panicked thoughts burbled up, and the only one he could catch long enough to read was, "I feel like I'm here and not here at the same time," which felt accurate enough as he lay on the ground and somehow loomed over it all.

The vantage point didn't provide him with a certain destination, but something ancient waited for him, and his ignorance was necessary to preserve him until he was ready to shirk it. It was inevitable. His destiny. His whole life swam through purpose as its ether, a curriculum that required rites to purify him and make him whole. It was time to wake up.

His insides were known to shift about, but promise though they might to escape entirely, they never succeeded. It turned out they just needed a little Adhikashara to finish the job.

His interior began to expand within him with enough force to indicate that it would be leaving him this time, to meld with the space around him and create a canvas out of the multiplicity of surrounding objects, a singular field of disembodied self, his bodily form nothing more than a system of values where differentiated space sat at the top of the pyramid as a ruler easily toppled by the broad wash of eternity enveloping it like a womb. His escaped interior pointed endlessly outward like an urchin's spines indicating in every direction, there I am, there I am, there I am, until this deference to the outside squished the central unified node between its thumb and forefinger and rolled it between them. It came apart like a loosened knot that disappears as it's untied.

His surroundings took on motion lines as though the whole scene were accelerating forward, reaching the speed of light in no time at all, and the three-dimensional world blurred and stretched in its trajectory through space-time such that the present moment became a single point occurring along the lengthened timeline of possible events, an infinite array of 3D frames, any one of which might be chosen by fate sweeping through, converted out of its potential and brought into being.

He was certain that he was dying, crossing the threshold from life to nothingness. But what awaited him was hardly oblivion.

As he changed his form, he tore his shirt in half like Clark Kent. It was *Carriers of the Cosmos 2: Beneath the Surface,* starring Lionel Lancet as The Clinger, whose superpower was clinging to the material world so that he enmeshed himself in the surfaces around him. It didn't lend itself to many action scenes like the first movie. There were more abstract impressions of the hero manifesting in various media.

Lionel's form integrated into a glint of oil spread thin on the surface of a murky puddle of water, almost hidden by the white Rolls Royce parked above. His outline distended in the arrhythmic drip of oil into the puddle, and swirling puffs of particulate road dirt were disquieted beneath the roiling concentric ripples.

He humbled himself to exist as the rising steam from the pot next to Constance and condensed onto the outside of the kitchen window. A gentle air current blew him over the house and the cliffs down to the shore below. He was grated within grains of sand, emulsified into the fibers of paper trash, ingrained into the wood of a picnic table, and surged within the hum of a streetlight.

A soft wind from the ocean bore against him, and he laced himself into its gusts, flutter kicking through water vapor. He rollicked within a plume of smoke and followed it down into a fire pit. Wafting in the swirl of char detritus, Lionel cooed in pleasure, but he froze at not hearing himself. He tried to speak, but he was silent.

Becoming the fire's tongues, he mouthed a cry and sent sparks around him. He cowered low in the cinders to an almost reverent submission as the realization of his present state took hold. He was an entity entirely dependent on things outside himself, objects in the world and only their appearances at that, contingent on light, horizons, peripheries, and penumbra. There were innumerable embodiments in the immensity of the world around him, and to all of it he relinquished his power.

He took to his malleable corporeality elegantly at first, having only recently apprehended being an ethereal floating thing. But it dawned on him that there might be no way out of being so disparately distributed into the surfaces of the world and smeared within the crevices of bending space-time. What could calm him? Advance him? Give him relief? Who could properly demarcate him from everything else when he deferred to other things for his being?

In his periphery, the light bent, and his surroundings closed in on him. Lionel found himself in an open toy chest. Christopher Hitchens loomed above him, rooting through the toys, looking for one he liked. Perhaps the religious figurines and Fisher-Price rosaries buried a child's chemistry set or plastic microscope. He tossed toys over his shoulder, one of which hit Plato on the head. Plato shoved Hitchens out of the way and reached into the toy chest. The toy he selected was Lionel, or whatever was left of him.

Plato brought him to a symbol that he had seen before. Lionel recognized it as the symbol Tomiina drew in the sand. Its edges scintillated, and the top of it was like a head which it began to thrash around in a tight figure-eight motion. It burst into silvery wisps and multiplied, sending symbols of an entire language about in shimmering purple, a dimension composed of pure forms, perfect geometric shapes that cast shafts of light below them.

Lionel tried to swim down toward material objects beneath the light shafts, but the forms pulled at him and kept him in their realm. Peering over the material world, he saw that the objects below were four-dimensional, a tangle of tube-like progressions of mass in time.

He followed his own tube-like form, snaking back from sipping the brew to the militia encampment, to Tony's, to his time with Tomiina, to Damian's abuse, accelerating all the way back to his blur of college, high school, and childhood. But an enormous hand snagged the timeline and stopped it.

The hand belonged to Aristotle. He had grasped spacetime, and Lionel landed in his father's car as a toddler. Strapped in his car seat, he looked at his father quizzically. Francis slowed their Audi in front of their house. He rocked his head to the side.

"We could do a couple more laps," Francis said, letting off the brake. "And don't tell your mother I said this..." he made eye contact with Lionel in the rearview mirror. "If someone presents themselves as a religious person, they just want you to think that they're special. This is a classic con. They make the promise that they are the friendliest, nicest, greatest person in the world, and people fall for it. Because people are sad and lonely and when they see someone else who isn't sad and lonely, they get a little hope. That energy is contagious."

Lionel stared out the window, sitting up taller to stare down the cliffs.

"The problem is that it doesn't work. It's a lie. And by conning everyone else, they start to believe the con, and it snowballs from there. Their ego inflates, and that feels like transcendence. And more people start to believe the hype. But it always falls apart since everyone else got the 'spirit' secondhand. Inevitably, everyone's sadness comes back, and everyone starts feeling lonely again, and they start to doubt the spiritual person who gave them confidence. And his addiction to power over people can't be satisfied by addressing just sadness and loneliness anymore. That was just the fix that got him hooked. And it's usually a him, by the way. So instead of addressing the sadness and loneliness of his followers' by attempting to lift them up again, he resents them. He sees it as proof of their disloyalty, and he loses interest in saving them. Or sometimes he kills them and fucks them. Not necessarily in that order."

They were back in front of their house again.

Francis looked into the rearview mirror at Lionel, who had fallen asleep. He beeped the horn, and Lionel flinched awake. Framed in the passenger window, Amelia strode out the front door in her beige Sunday's best.

The waves crashed into the rocky beach at the base of the cliffs beneath the Wayfarer's Chapel as they took their seats inside.

Plato came up behind Aristotle and goosed him, which made him lose his grip on the timeline. It began rushing back again, and as the tide receded, Lionel came out of his mother's womb in the hospital room, and her past stretched far back as well, along with Francis's. Their pasts were entwined until they separated and snaked off into their mothers and so on, an infinite braid of being, all wrapped within itself.

Zooming out further, he saw a more broadened scope than anyone could without getting a little nauseated, or maybe it was just the brew. He witnessed societies rise, spread themselves like mold, and fall, over and over again, stretching far out of view into the future and deep into the distant past.

He bore witness to history, a procession of darkness sweeping across the land, cold and indifferent to any end of an era. Lionel watched people machine-gunned in trenches, loaded into train cars, gassed, and swept by the eviscerating wall of a nuclear blast, and the world continued to hurdle and turn, and time continued forward without any savior dropping down to bring a stop to it. And more terror awaited those who escaped, having to carry on knowing that there was more to come. History wasn't finished yet.

From this perspective, any talk of cause and effect became laughable. Nothing was the cause of anything else. Time never sat still long enough for the fallout from the big bang to wear off and give a fresh start and a clean slate. And nothing of himself was his own. It was all inherited, generation after generation, from thousands of years ago, all the way back to the first man possessed with darkness, or before that, from an animalistic forerunner to the Homo sapiens who used darkness to survive lest they become prey, and they would pass down this darkness, this angry, sullen trajectory, gathering momentum toward its next unknowing beneficiary.

A flash of pink darted behind him, and Lionel drifted toward it. Perhaps it was just another geometric form. Something tapped him on his disembodied shoulder, and he spun around, catching a glimpse of the same pink flash. Turning back, he came face to face with a pink, elephant-headed being.

Ganesha flourished his hands ironically, like "spooky, I know." He made little fuss about his entrance in spite of Lionel's cowering in fear. Apprehending Ganesha proved to be an insurmountable obstacle. Ganesha spoke without moving his mouth. "You cannot stay here. But you cannot return either."

Ganesha shoved him downward, and Lionel fell like the floor gave out. He landed suspended between the world of forms and material objects. Plato and Aristotle embraced and unified. The crown of Lionel's head seared with pain, and blood dripped into his eyes. Stigmata appeared in each of his hands and feet. He became Jesus, material and divine at once.

In his infinite grace and love, Lionel pondered Tomiina, Damian, Melanie, Constance, his father, his grandfather, and at last, his mother who abandoned him, leaving a hole in his heart that he buried so deeply he didn't know it was there. He forgave them and loved them.

"They know not what they do."

Chapter 19

Lionel ascended and returned, floating down the second half of his parabolic arc like an angel descending to earth to share the good news. Time moved against his bodily form like a cool breeze gently carrying a leaf. His path wended, and at each change in direction he relented to forces beyond him, revering the space he swam through with unfamiliar deftness. A smile appeared on his face at rest.

Constance and Tony enjoyed his newfound deliberate eye contact, his pupils, still wide in the comedown, drinking them in. The slow rhythm of the distant waves reminded him of something beyond words, the earthly signs that shone down from a withdrawn expanse. He was content to be cradled within it, basking in the sunlit yard. Morning came when he and reality were not on speaking terms, but it greeted him warmly now.

Waving his hands in front of his face, he regarded them as outgrowths of his will, and his feet responded to his commands as if by magic. Breathing revealed itself as a fascinating opportunity. Before, parked in front of his computer for hours at a time, his breathing would be reduced to imperceptibly sipping at the body soil enriched air that settled around him. Cooler air entered now and felt massive, hitting the back of his throat like a refreshing glass of water.

But it wasn't all pleasant. Visiting interdimensional entities and peering behind the curtain of the material world to stare into the boundless expanse of infinity was terrifying. Among the myriad sensations that occurred as the Adhikashara digested in his gut was impending doom. Nor was it vague about what would happen. The moment it hit his stomach, it promised to erase him, to smear him against space until he passed through it like oil through cheesecloth. His interior was always unreliable, but Adhikashara gave it the proper motivation to up and leave, adjusting his temperature to match the air around him so the boundaries of his body melted away.

Lionel was unwilling, to say the least. It offered to take him quietly, but after his significant resistance, it dragged him with his fingernails splintering, clawing against the familiar world of objects.

So was he transformed? Perhaps. Would it be permanent? Time would tell. But his newfound lightness was mostly an expression of relief at being back on earth. It was nice knowing that gravity reliably pulled at him and that objects stayed put unless met with an outside force. He got a front-row seat to the absence that lurked beyond the surfaces that objects showed him, and he was perfectly happy to let that carry on beyond his purview. He already struggled with bullies on the material plane, and there was little to be gained by standing up to everything trying to boss him around on the other side.

Besides, he was a supernatural being now. Or he had always been, but now he was privy to that information. He likely couldn't perform miracles or raise the dead, but he had insight, the right view of the world. This was better than knowledge. What use is a fact? Simple trivia missed the forest for the trees. Lionel had the proper frame, and anything that fell within it became animated with forces beyond mere appearances. He could see things as they really were because he saw what he really was, a shard of the godhead, a spark shot off the molten divinity of the universe, struck by a cosmic blacksmith's mallet of love.

Constance touched her hand to Lionel's shoulder. He welcomed it. She prepared breakfast, and after he and Tony proved they were back in their bodies, they drifted slowly to the table on the porch. Butter melted down a stack of pancakes, and golden brown hash potatoes lay in a mound beneath eggs, sunny side up. Sunlight passed through the bottle of syrup and gave it an amber glow. Constance set out glass plates decorated with farmers tilling land encircled by flowers.

They sat at the table, but Lionel barely touched his food. His stomach was comfortably empty, and the food satisfied something in him by simply appearing in his visual field. The steam rising off everything seemed to indicate an internal essence emerging from the meal that was inherently positive. He sniffed slowly to appreciate the aroma but more so to bring its aura inside himself.

"There was, like, an alien dude who stared at me, and he had three heads, and each of them was a different aspect of myself," said Tony. "One was me as the performer, and that head was making silly faces, and the head on the other side was the director, and he was kinda leaning back, checking me out and contemplating, but the one in the middle was blank, there was no face..."

Lionel half-listened. He nodded at appropriate times and raised his eyebrows in reaction. But it was clear to him that Tony misinterpreted his experience. Surely the "alien" he met was no alien at all but his own divinity. Lionel perceived this numinous aspect as though it were reflected in the light in his eyes. Constance listened to Tony's account, and Lionel expected her to break and reveal that she saw it as well and was only waiting for him to finish so she could correct him. But neither seemed to be willing to say it—that here were gathered three divine beings carrying on like regular people.

When Tony finished, Lionel asked him leadingly, "So the third head, what was that aspect of yourself?"

"I don't know, man. That was only a little part of it. I spent most my time chillin' with the tree goddess," said Tony, leaning back in his chair. "What did you think of her?"

Lionel was puzzled.

"It can take several ceremonies to meet her," said Constance. "She will show herself when you're ready."

"Man," said Tony, getting choked up. "It made me think of my mother. And my sister. And all the women in the industry. And how we make it all about the body, you know? Like, I never felt how that was the wrong path. But I've got to make some changes, you know? I think I need to leave the industry. I need to get a steady job, and I'm thinking I'm gonna go to church."

"That's beautiful, Tony," said Constance.

"And it's crazy but I think I need to be a father," said Tony, and he burst into tears. Constance brought her hand to Tony's back.

Lionel smiled patiently. He forked a bite of pancakes into his mouth, but his body didn't want it. Pretending to be occupied, he averted his eyes to the houses in the hills above. How many people were up there, getting up and going to work or living out their retirement oblivious to their true nature? Lionel pitied them.

Lionel was alarmed when he noticed Constance was looking at him. She expected nothing, simply taking him in. Still, he felt compelled to share his revelations. But there was a growing sense he had done it wrong. There was no tree goddess to be seen in his journey. The only beings he saw were men. Perhaps Tony and Constance were both wrong.

"I saw the tree goddess," said Lionel. Constance smiled at him, brushing tears off Tony's face. "She made me realize that kindness is the answer."

His phone vibrated in his pocket.

"It's Tomiina," said Lionel. "Should I answer it?"

"Of course," said Tony, sitting up.

"I don't know if I should."

"It's your choice," said Constance. "But whatever you decide, do it out of love, not anger or fear."

Lionel looked into Constance's eyes. Beyond her dark irises and calm gaze was sadness for him that one day he would die. It appeared to him as though it were written on her face. He knew this immediately to be love and answered his phone to escape from it.

"Hello?"

"Hey... It's me," said Tomiina. "Can I see you?"

"Yeah," said Lionel, grabbing a clump of his hair. "When works for you?"

"Can you meet tonight?"

"Yes."

"Come to the hotel lobby."

"Okay. I think I'm in love with you."

Tony and Constance exchanged horrified glances and shook their heads, mouthing no.

"She hung up," said Lionel, bringing the phone away from his ear. "I don't think she heard me."

"Thank god," said Tony.

"Approach it more casually," said Constance. "No grand declarations."

"Right," said Lionel.

He excused himself to use the restroom, but he didn't have to go. He looked at himself in the mirror and saw a god staring back at him.

Chapter 20

Even though Lionel didn't get to meet the tree goddess, the psychedelic brew did a good job of clearing him of some of his notions. His resentment for Tomiina was gone. It seemed unlikely that a religious cult was trying to kill him. Wouldn't they have done it already? It must have been a projection stemming from his atheism, which vanished as well. He was still working out the details of his new belief system, which involved some sort of pantheism rooted in the tension between Plato and Aristotle. He would have to brush up on both thinkers. Sometimes, he mixed them up.

Lionel started to consider Damian as a hurt child whose divinity was buried under pain and a new plastic face. The lawsuits were still on, and Damian's involvement was still to be determined, but Lionel knew he could reach him with a little kindness and vulnerability. If he approached it openly and honestly, everything would work out. If that didn't work, surely his newfound divinity would shine through in some influential way. He pondered for a moment that he should start a podcast.

Lionel loaded boxes of Adhikashara into Tony's Rolls Royce, as Tony said goodbye to Constance inside. She came out the front door to send them off and called something to Lionel which he didn't hear. At Tony's, Lionel stepped one foot inside before it became clear what he had to do.

Nothing about the interior of Tony's house changed. The same grand entryway led to the same sitting room, and the guest room he stayed in was just as he left it. But beyond the luxurious appearance of what might have been his new digs persisted the feeling that he was running away from his responsibilities. He was not homeless. He had never been. The villa at the Hotel Bellehaven was in his name. And Tomiina never cut ties. She still wanted to see him. As for the lawsuits, he had been hoping they would disappear if he ignored them long enough, but they persisted just like the divinity within him.

"Let me give you something at least," said Tony as Lionel got in his car.

Tony disappeared into his house and returned with Marcus who wore a yellow tracksuit. In Marcus's hands was the Exorcist, and he loaded it into Lionel's back seat.

Lionel rocked his head side to side sucking air between his teeth.

"It's not up for debate," said Tony.

Lionel shrugged. He and Tony clasped hands through the open window.

At the Hotel Bellehaven, Lionel carried himself slowly across the grounds feeling the setting sun on his face. He held his head high not to signal anything but because it felt good to broaden his view. There wasn't much to see with his head down all the time. His vision seemed to illuminate the world around him, summoning everything he looked at into existence.

He didn't believe this per se, but perhaps his visual field was an evolutionary adaptation that affected his environment like a beaver's evolved capacity to build a dam. The beaver dam was an expression of evolution that extended beyond the beaver itself, and his visual field did the same, he reasoned. Didn't his vision delineate the boundaries of his experience and actualize color and light by looking at it? He would have to run that one by Dawkins. Lionel didn't even begin to try to square his recent experience with the perspective of his favorite atheists. At one moment, he could have sworn he saw the outline of the hotel ripple in response to his eyesight observing it.

It occurred to him that he should whistle. He blew air through his lips, but no sound came out.

To the north, a golfer took her time squaring up for a practice swing, holding the wedge far from striking distance. A cigar rested between her lips. It went out, and she examined the burnt end, cursing. Lionel, oblivious, crossed the green, and she froze. She put the cigar back in her mouth and pointed the hidden camera in her lapel at him to ensure he was in frame.

Lionel's blissful walk brought him to the edge of the Hotel Bellehaven seal in the grass, and he stopped short of tramping over it. Rounding its perimeter instead, he proceeded, and a patch of grass seemed to emerge out of nowhere, and he tripped on it. He slowly got back to his feet.

It was mostly empty inside the lobby, and Lionel smiled at a middle-aged man who had a deep, brown suntan from years of surfing and scars of long, parallel scratch marks on his face. The man avoided his eyes and seated himself next to two of his friends.

Lionel stationed himself in front of the pillar where he used to attend the lobby. He didn't look like an employee, just a white guy in a dashiki and gym shorts beaming at everyone.

Before long, Tomiina emerged from the northern hall as though his presence called her there. In actuality, they had agreed to meet in the lobby.

Instantly, Lionel knew that his past years of life were a somnambulant interim in which he was deluded and in the dark. It was all necessary, preparation for this moment with her. He never would have believed it before. Déjà vu rang through him along with the feeling that forces beyond him made him forget the portent of their shared space so that it would hit him harder when he remembered.

His habit of feebly dismantling anything too emotionally demanding with empty rationalizations and misplaced applications of logic went impotent and became foreign to him in light of the hollow widening within him and the indecipherable elsewhere that Tomiina's form invited him toward, loud and incoherent like noise. Her appearance called to him coyly, demanding from him an ascent from the foothold of appearances and objects whether his vision created them or not.

Lionel put his arms out like Christ welcoming his flock. She hadn't noticed him yet and went into the women's restroom. He crossed the lobby and waited outside the door. When she came out, he was leaning against the wall with his knee bent like the Marlboro man.

"Tomiina," he said airily.

Tomiina flinched and clasped a hand to her chest.

"Oh my god." Shifting, she hugged him. "It's good to see you."

"I know I was on a bad path."

"Oh, we're doing this right here?"

"I knew I put a lot on you, and I'm sorry," said Lionel. "The truth is... what that's just it, I thought I knew the truth. I thought that's all I was, a truth machine. And I thought I knew everything. But I was wrong. That's right. I was wrong. I, Lionel Lancet, was wrong. And I've been working on myself a lot in the past few days."

"That's great, Lionel–"

"Actually, I'm just barely getting started, if you could let me finish..."

"Sure," said Tomiina, looking at her hands. Her eyes seemed grave and ancient. Lionel quivered, feeling that the two of them were enacting something eternal, a moment elevated to join the ranks of an ever-repeating cosmic expression of love.

"I had a bit of a wild experience. It was on a drug, I admit. But it was real. Or it was meaningful, at least. I don't know what 'real' is," said Lionel. "At the beginning of time, our souls were conjoined. We were gods. Or God. We still are, really. But we forgot when we were born and put into bodies. We forgot our unity and divinity and how we're connected, to each other and to everything else. And we think we're individual selves, but I woke up. I remembered everything." Tears streamed down his cheeks, but his eyes were wide open and locked on Tomiina. "And it's my calling to come to earth wake you up and remind you of what you really are so we can unite again."

Tomiina stared back at him with her mouth slightly opened.

"I know," Lionel said. "You should have seen my face when I found out. We're shards of God, and we're supposed to unite. We have the chance to be together forever. I know it. Do you remember?" He searched her face for recognition. "Do you remember, Tomiina?" She put a hand over her mouth and shook her head. He sighed heavily, saying, "We've been at it this way since the beginning of time."

Everything went dark before Lionel realized that the mouth of a long canvas bag slipped over his head. The inside smelled like detergent. Someone pushed him to the ground, and the bag swallowed him whole. He struggled feebly inside as a drawstring tightened beneath his feet. They began to drag him.

Friction from the canvas moving against the carpet created warmth beneath him. He foolishly tried to stand up inside the bag. When that didn't work, he kicked his feet against the opening. A sharp blow from the outside put a stop to that, and he yelped. They dragged him in a straight line, changed direction, and dragged him some more, and before long they lifted the end of the bag at his feet. His hip collided with something hard, which he met with a moan. Upon a second collision with something at a right angle to the first, Lionel realized they were dragging him up a set of stairs. All of his weight bore down, and the hard corners of the stairs scraped and dug into him like a violent deep tissue massage.

When he was on even ground again, they dumped him out of the bag. Bright lights beamed down on him, hanging from a catwalk. Lionel lay center stage in the Beaumont Theater. His captors grabbed him and wrestled his flailing body into a chair, and they tied him to it with synthetic rope. As his eyes adjusted, a dining room table materialized in front of him with a simple candelabra and tablecloth.

Across from him was Damian's stiff, bloated face. To his left sat Lee Furnival. The three men who dragged and bound him posted up in a line, stage left. One of them was the man Lionel smiled at in the lobby. Their sunburns were deep and brown.

For a moment, they all looked at Lionel dispassionately. Tears poured down his face and made the candlelight stretch out into stars.

"We will proceed with your permission, Mr. President," said Lee Furnival.

Lionel was too dumbfounded to respond. Everyone looked at him for his go-ahead. Damian smoothed his hair.

"We cannot begin without your permission," said Damian sharply. Lowering his voice, he said, "Come on, Lovely Lionel."

Lionel shook his head. Damian stood, scooting his chair back with a large scraping sound, and crossed to Lionel. He clasped Lionel's face and jerked his head up and down in a nodding motion.

Damian returned to his seat with an exasperated sigh.

"Now in session is the official sacrificial meeting for the Fiduciary Royalties Association for United Donors," said Damian. "Thank you all for taking the time out of your schedules, and please remember to block out the first Thursday in June for our annual luncheon. Also if you haven't yet, submit your name to me for the Secret Santa. And please, don't submit if you're not going to buy a gift. I'm looking at you, Lee."

Lee hunched and rolled his eyes.

The rope binding Lionel's arms, chest, and legs to the chair prevented his movement and sufficient breathing. He tried to twist his arms out of the tightly wrapped rope, but it only dug into his skin. The candle flames danced in front of him, rising from their wicks, long and thin. Almost imperceptible smoke coiled out of the top of each flame tip. He could swear the flames moved in synchronicity with the waves of anxiety passing through him like a toxin.

Sweat dripped down Lee Furnival's nose and onto the packet of papers that lay in front of him. He cleared his throat and gestured with his palm up. "We do what we do out of duty."

Everyone but Lionel repeated after him, "We do what we do out of duty."

"A necessity incorporated out of natural paternal contempt..."

"A necessity incorporated out of natural paternal contempt..."

"For the childish want to be coddled..."

"For the childish want to be coddled..."

"For the silence of our animalism..."

"For the silence of our animalism..."

"For the nameless expanse the world is reduced to in our sleep..."

"For the nameless expanse the world is reduced to in our sleep..."

"For the undifferentiated land..."

"For the undifferentiated land..."

"For the lame thrashing of body without the direction of will..."

"For the lame thrashing of body without the direction of will..."

"For the empty nowhere between earth and sky..."

"For the empty nowhere between earth and sky..."

"For the thief who would steal our boon..."

"For the thief who would steal our boon..."

"For the faulty scales weighted toward want over reason..."

"For the faulty scales weighted toward want over reason..."

"For the bright shining eyes that would cast evil wherever they look..."

"For the bright shining eyes that would cast evil wherever they look..."

Lee looked away from the papers, reciting from memory, "Lo! Another offering brought to release essence into the ether. May he carry the cosmos to the gate of death and pave a way through it for all he will leave behind."

The rest of the men said, "It shall be done."

The men standing around the table stomped their feet in unison three times. Damian and Lee rose, and Lionel braced himself as everyone came at him at once.

One of the sunburned men tilted Lionel's chair back, and the two others came on either side of him to hold his head still.

Lee Furnival withdrew a serpent-handled dagger and a set of pliers. He handed the pliers to Damian, who drew them toward Lionel's fearful mouth.

Lionel, no longer an atheist but certainly in a foxhole, made a desperate internal plea expressed as a flash of expectant adrenaline for something to save him and forgive him for his wrongdoings. He knew it would have to come out of another dimension, a metaphysical *deus ex machina* that would reveal itself to have been waiting in the wings, having guided him in a navigable trajectory to the brink of death only to save him and to confirm that there was something up there watching over him.

At the pace that the timeline slackened to, Lionel indulged in further speculation that this savior would be an agent of fate that could thwart his grandfather's foundation that conspired after all to humiliate and sacrifice him, tax-free.

All proof that time continued to move vanished, and the scene hung statically, a variation on a portrait that appeared throughout human history of older generations rearing to sacrifice the youth to appease forces that might just operate on their own if they had a little faith instead of hedging risk with rituals and totems. The meeting stretched beyond the space of the theater and revealed itself as a cross-section of a broad object of which each piece was shaped like the whole. Lionel, as just a little part of it, furrowed his brow, confused as ever at his surroundings. For all their elevated portent and congruence with extra-dimensional transcendence, the inert wood of the stage insisted upon itself in his field of view. And in spite of the cinematic pace with which Damian reached the pliers at him, there was something ugly and unstylish about his movement. The candles went out.

With the gods indifferent to him, who was this that should save him now? Melanie Bobbers entered from stage left with a police officer, the camera in her lapel full of surprised faces. She stopped in a well-lit section of the stage.

"Sorry to crash the party," said Melanie. "Hope you don't mind I brought a plus one."

What unfolded after such a dramatic entrance amounted to a rather anticlimactic arrest of the members of the Fiduciary Royalties Association for United Donors for the attempted murder of their president, Lionel Lancet. With only one officer, who was a short, portly man, breathing heavily, scrambling around trying to cuff everyone, the arrest took a long time, and he had to call backup so that there would be more room to haul everyone away.

As one of the sunburned men got cuffed, Melanie shoved the camera in his face, and said, "This is the asshole who tore out my tooth. He's a mediocre surfer at best." He kept his face blank as the cop led him away.

Melanie untied Lionel and helped him to the edge of the stage, draping a blanket over him like a freed hostage at the end of an action movie. But instead of paramedics rushing around and relieved smiles after such a close call, it was just Lionel and Melanie Bobbers sharing a silence. She was a little disappointed she didn't catch him doing something nefarious. The only crime that had been committed was everyone attempting to yank Lionel's teeth out and stab him with a dagger, which was illegal in all fifty states.

Lionel slowly looked up at her. From the perspective of her lapel camera, he looked like a scared child seeking reassurance from his mother, blinking back tears. He hugged Melanie and cried, eyes closed, his face pressed against the camera lens. After a moment of resistance, she held him, and with a closed mouth she touched her tongue to her false tooth.

The theater loomed large around Lionel. Everyone else had left. Lionel rose from the edge of the stage and walked into the wing, stage left. Nothing around him seemed real. Even his body felt fraudulent. Lionel began to ascend the ladder up to the prop loft, but halfway up, he stopped. The edges of his field of view softened and faded into darkness on every side. He was sandwiched between the ground, which vanished from sight, and the unknown, potential space above. This limbo on wooden rungs afforded him a brief respite from anything committal. The teeth embedded in the wood above might not exist as long as he didn't check to see if they had ever actually been there.

He was right about the foundation's attempt to sacrifice him. But figuring out the rest was a wash. Perhaps there was some logic to the foundation's ideology of death, but it was hidden from him. Melanie Bobbers had been dogging him, but she also saved him. Was she right about him? What had she even accused him of? The lawsuit was still on, but he never cleared up just what it was about.

And Tomiina. What was her role in all of this? There, between the ground and prop loft, he didn't have to decide. He could rest. His exhaustion carved at him from the inside, taxing his muscles at the slightest movement. Clinging to the ladder's rungs, he listened to the empty space around him, projecting a resonant tone that didn't exist, pretending to warm the space with imaginary vibration. The yellow-purple color of bruises occupied the void in his closed eyes and shifted about like clouds.

Part III
The Trial

Chapter 21

Soon after Lionel's deposition, Melanie Bobbers posted the audio of the Lunada Bay Boys' attempt to sacrifice her, and *Little Miss ProseCute* blew up. She landed a spot on *SoC(i)al Media Monthly*'s "Top 10 Badass Women" list, which judiciously shirked any ordinal ranking so as to celebrate the ten selected women equally. Letters of support poured into her Highland Park office, along with a few death threats, but they only made her stand taller. It was usually considered bad form for a prosecuting attorney to indulge in the fanfare before a big trial, but she justified her YouTube interviews and talk show appearances as an empowering message to young women. And as long as she didn't mention the specifics of her case against Lionel Lancet, she was in the clear.

She got a brand new wardrobe for her media appearances, stylish pantsuits and blazer/slacks combos. She decided on a simple skirt and overcoat, all black, for Lionel's trial. Looking in the full-length mirror in her office, adjusting her sleeves, Melanie pursed her lips and narrowed her eyes. Her partner popped her head into the frame and said, "You look like a spy."

"I was going more for Satan," said Melanie.

Lionel managed to assemble an outfit that made him look like a legacy kid at a prep school bound for a finance job on Wall Street: a navy blue sport coat over a white Oxford dress shirt, a conservative red striped tie, and brown chinos.

He sat alone on his side of the courtroom, having chosen to represent himself, against all common sense. Constance and Tony sat behind him. The presiding judge was the Honorable Cynthia Dimikitinin, a no-nonsense septuagenarian who missed her lunch that day.

THE UNITED STATES   CaseNo. BC4351893

          Plaintiff

   vs.

LIONEL LANCET

          Defendant

SUPERIOR COURT OF THE STATE OF CALIFORNIA

COUNTY OF LOS ANGELES

          TRIAL TRANSCRIPT, taken at 1:10
P.M., Thursday, September 9, 2016, at 111 N
Hill Street, Los Angeles, California, before
Shawntese Bordel, C&R 3255, rpr, pursuant to
Notice.

PROCEEDINGS

THE COURT: Ms. Bobbers, you may proceed.

MS. BOBBERS: Now calling to the stand, Damian Radic. Tell me, Mr. Radic, what was Mr. Lancet's role in the Fiduciary Royalties Association for United Donors?

MR. RADIC: President.

MR. LANCET: Objection.

THE COURT: What is your objection, Mr. Lancet?

MR. LANCET: That's not even true.

THE COURT: That's not how this works, Mr. Lancet.

MR. RADIC: It is true.

MR. LANCET: But it's not fair.

THE COURT: We will maintain a sense of decorum in this courtroom. You will have your time to speak, Mr. Lancet.

MS. BOBBERS: What was your role in the foundation, Mr. Radic?

MR. RADIC: I plead the fifth.

MS. BOBBERS: I can assure you that you are not on trial today. We just need to establish your personal and professional proximity to Mr. Lancet. How do you know Mr. Lancet?

MR. RADIC: He worked under me at the Hotel Bellehaven.

MS. BOBBERS: How was his performance as an employee?

MR. RADIC: Spectacular. He knew what I wanted before I said anything. It was like he was pulling all the strings.

MS. BOBBERS: Is it your opinion that Lionel, as President of the Fiduciary Royalties Association for United Donors, led the foundation in this similarly dominant capacity?

MR. RADIC: Absolutely. He was in charge of everything and made all the important decisions.

MS. BOBBERS: But he didn't orchestrate his own attempted murder, correct?

MR. RADIC: Unless it was a ploy.

MS. BOBBERS: Could you expound?

MR. RADIC: It would certainly make him look innocent of the other attempts to sacrifice people if it looked like he himself was about to be sacrificed. That's his whole thing: pretending to be harmless. But there is a lot of darkness in him.

MS. BOBBERS: I see. To clarify, are you suggesting Lionel orchestrated the attempts to murder the victims of the foundation in a series of religious sacrifices?

MR. RADIC: Yes.

MS. BOBBERS: And you yourself participated in these, did you not?

MR. RADIC: I plead the fifth.

MS. BOBBERS: I have no further questions.

————

THE COURT: Mr. Lancet, you may now question Mr. Radic.

MR. LANCET: Damian. Is it the truth that you just said I was a good employee?

MR. RADIC: Yes.

MR. LANCET: 'Spectacular,' I think you said. But were you not the one who demoted me more than once for being incompetent?

MR. RADIC: No.

MR. LANCET: But you did.

MS. BOBBERS: Objection. Leading the witness.

THE COURT: Sustained.

MR. RADIC: When did I do that?

MR. LANCET: Order. I'll ask the questions, thank you.

THE COURT: You don't get to say order, Mr. Lancet. That's my job.

MR. LANCET: I'm sorry, your honor.

THE COURT: You may proceed.

MR. LANCET: Was I not the one who had a panic attack and took off my shirt when you asked me to clean every surface in the hotel?

MR. RADIC: Not that I recall.

MR. LANCET: Oh, come on. I was taking my shirt off all the time.

THE COURT: Please proceed with your line of questioning, Mr. Lancet.

MR. LANCET: Okay. What about when I delivered those documents to the wrong address? Was I not the one who screwed that up too? I'm gonna need a full answer, in words.

MR. RADIC: That might have happened. Everyone makes mistakes. I don't have time to keep track of them all.

MR. LANCET: But do you recall that it was I who was the one who got that document notarized and stomped all over the hotel seal on the ground? Or was it not?

MR. RADIC: I don't recall.

MR. LANCET: Did you or did you not go on vacation when I worked at the Hotel Bellehaven?

MR. RADIC: I did.

MR. LANCET: Okay, now we're getting somewhere. Where did you go?

MR. RADIC: My girlfriend and I went to Cabo.

MR. LANCET: Girlfriend?

MR. RADIC: Yes. We've been together for five years.

MR. LANCET: I see. I wasn't aware. I'm just going to come out and ask. Did you try to pin these lawsuits on me? Or did you not?

MR. RADIC: I did not.

MR. LANCET: But you did try to murder me, didn't you?

MR. RADIC: No.

MR. LANCET: Yes, you did.

MR. RADIC: No, I didn't.

MS. BOBBERS: Objection. Asked and answered.

THE COURT: Sustained. Mr. Lancet, do you have any more questions?

MR. LANCET: I guess not. I just thought taking an oath to tell the truth used to mean something.

THE COURT: Please return to your seat.

———

MS. BOBBERS: Now calling to the stand Mr. Lee Furnival. Mr. Furnival, what was Mr. Lancet's role in the Fiduciary Royalties Association for United Donors?

MR. FURNIVAL: President. It's all in the paperwork.

MS. BOBBERS: Could you describe your relationship to the defendant's foundation?

MR. FURNIVAL: I was formerly their lawyer.

MS. BOBBERS: I see. When did you part ways?

MR. FURNIVAL: Shortly after Art Lancet died.

MS. BOBBERS: That's correct. In fact, it seems it was Mr. Lancet, Lionel Lancet that is, who released you from your position.

MR. LANCET: What the heck?

THE COURT: Mr. Lancet, your outbursts are unwelcome in this court. I will have you removed if you keep this up.

MR. LANCET: But I didn't do that!

THE COURT: Order!

MS. BOBBERS: I'd like to draw the court's attention to this document. Mr. Furnival, as a lawyer, could you tell me what this document is?

MR. FURNIVAL: This is a Release of All Claims.

MS. BOBBERS: Could you read the document for the court?

MR. FURNIVAL: Certainly. 'I Lionel Lancet, President of the Fiduciary Royalties Association for United Donors absolve Mr. Lee Furnival from any and all claims arising out of Mr. Furnival's representation of our foundation.'

MS. BOBBERS: And that signature, on the bottom, whose is that?

MR. FURNIVAL: That is Mr. Lancet's signature.

MS. BOBBERS: Lionel Lancet's?

MR. FURNIVAL: Yes.

MS. BOBBERS: Thank you, Mr. Furnival. I'd like to show one more document. In your legal expertise, could you tell us what document this is?

MR. FURNIVAL: This is a Transfer of Assets.

MS. BOBBERS: Okay, and where is this money being transferred, according to this document?

MR. FURNIVAL: It appears to be an account in the Cayman Islands.

MS. BOBBERS: Fascinating. What do you know about the Cayman Islands?

MR. FURNIVAL: They're a series of small islands south of Cuba.

MS. BOBBERS: Yes, they are. Perhaps I should rephrase. Could you hazard a guess as to why Mr. Lancet chose the Cayman Islands?

MR. FURNIVAL: If I'm not mistaken, the Cayman Islands are tax neutral.

MS. BOBBERS: You are not mistaken, Mr. Furnival. And I'll add that this is relatively common knowledge, but I appreciate your caution. We wouldn't want to say anything too damning. Do you know who owns this account?

MR. FURNIVAL: I do not.

MS. BOBBERS: Do you own this account?

MR. FURNIVAL: No.

MS. BOBBERS: Does Mr. Lancet own this account?

MR. FURNIVAL: Not that I'm aware of.

MS. BOBBERS: Okay. Could you read the signature at the bottom of this document?

MR. FURNIVAL: There are two.

MS. BOBBERS: Yes, it appears one belongs to a Notary Public in Santa Monica. Could you please read the other?

MR. FURNIVAL: It says Lionel Lancet.

MS. BOBBERS: So with his signature on your Release of All Claims document and the notarized Transfer of Assets, it's safe to say that Mr. Lancet had an active role in the foundation. Is that correct?

MR. FURNIVAL: Yes.

MS. BOBBERS: To what degree did Mr. Lancet participate in the religious aspects of the foundation?

MR. FURNIVAL: What exactly?

MS. BOBBERS: The drugs? The ritual sacrifice? Tearing out people's teeth?

MR. FURNIVAL: I plead the fifth.

MS. BOBBERS: I actually became the target of one of the rituals, and thanks to these surfing legs, I managed to escape. But I also saw you trying to do the same to Mr. Lancet here, do you remember that?

MR. FURNIVAL: Uh, I'm afraid I don't recall.

MS. BOBBERS: Do you recall me crashing the party and having you arrested?

MR. FURNIVAL: I plead the fifth.

MS. BOBBERS: I will ask you again, to what degree was Lionel involved in the religious aspects of the foundation?

MR. FURNIVAL: I plead the fifth.

MS. BOBBERS: I have no further questions.

———

MR. LANCET: I feel betrayed, Lee. It seems like you got me to sign that document when we met on Santa Monica Pier.

THE COURT: Mr. Lancet. This is your time to question Mr. Furnival, not opine on the details of the case.

MR. LANCET: Thank you, your honor. I'm getting there. It seems, Mr. Furnival, like you tricked me into signing that claims document. Does it not?

MR. FURNIVAL: No.

MR. LANCET: Okay, so you "didn't." But you did try to murder me, didn't you?

MR. FURNIVAL: No.

MR. LANCET: Mr. Furnival, how are we supposed to have a rational debate if you can't even be honest?

MR. FURNIVAL: I don't believe this is a debate, Mr. Lancet.

MR. LANCET: I guess that's fair. But I will say that this impropriety is irrational. And it's unwelcome in this court.

THE COURT: Mr. Lancet, are you—

MR. LANCET: I just wanted to give Mr. Furnival a chance to think about his answers really carefully. Do you recall the document that Ms. Bobbers mentioned? The transfer of assets?

MR. FURNIVAL: Yes.

MR. LANCET: What was all that about?

MR. FURNIVAL: I'm not sure. I just saw it for the first time.

MR. LANCET: It seems that Damian, Mr. Radic that is, sent me to notarize that document. Correct?

MR. FURNIVAL: I don't know.

MR. LANCET: Why do you think he did that?

MR. FURNIVAL: I have no idea. You should have asked him when you were questioning him.

MR. LANCET: Well, if I'd thought of that… You know what, never mind. If you're not going to cooperate, I have no further questions. And just so everyone knows, I didn't know anything about those documents.

THE COURT: Mr. Lancet, you will respect the proceedings of this court, or I will hold you in contempt.

MR. LANCET: My bad.

————

MS. BOBBERS: Now calling to the stand, Mr. Anthony Motion. Mr. Motion, how do you know Mr. Lancet?

MR. MOTION: We met when he dropped a delivery at my house by mistake.

MS. BOBBERS: And what was the delivery?

MR. MOTION: It was a lot of documents.

MS. BOBBERS: What was in those documents?

MR. MOTION: There was a lot. There were like ten boxes.

MS. BOBBERS: Was Mr. Lancet attempting to get rid of them?

MR. MOTION: I think it was a legit accident.

MS. BOBBERS: Okay. What is your profession, Mr. Motion?

MR. MOTION: I'm in between jobs right now, but I was in the entertainment industry.

MS. BOBBERS: For what kind of projects?

MR. MOTION: Adult entertainment. But I left the industry. I'm trying to find work that's more traditional.

MS. BOBBERS: Okay. And beyond Lionel dropping the documents off at your house by mistake, did you have any other interaction with him?

MR. MOTION: He came back to pick up the documents. And he also came to me looking for help.

MS. BOBBERS: What did he need help with?

MR. MOTION: He was under the impression people were trying to kill him.

MS. BOBBERS: I see. And did you help Mr. Lancet?

MR. MOTION: I let him stay at my place.

MS. BOBBERS: Did the two of you leave at all?

MR. MOTION: We uh, we left to get some stuff, and went down to Palos Verdes.

MS. BOBBERS: Okay, and what stuff did you get?

MR. MOTION: I plead the fifth.

MS. BOBBERS: Do you have a criminal history?

MR. MOTION: Why'd you ask me that?

MS. BOBBERS: Just—It just came to mind.

MR. MOTION: You didn't ask anybody else that.

MS. BOBBERS: You're right. I apologize, Mr. Motion. And I acknowledge that the question might have offended you as a black man.

MR. MOTION: That don't make it better.

MS. BOBBERS: I apologize. Now, speaking of, did Mr. Lancet ever say or do anything that indicated that he held prejudices against certain groups of people?

MR. MOTION: He was having some issues with the ladies. I think he's a little antisemitic too.

MS. BOBBERS: I have no further questions.

MR. MOTION: He didn't say anything about black people.

MS. BOBBERS: Thank you for your time, Mr. Motion.

MR. MOTION: But we were the first Semitic people, you know. So I guess by extension he was racist in that way.

MS. BOBBERS: No further questions.

MR. MOTION: You know, America was actually discovered by Africans.

———

THE COURT: Mr. Lancet, get on with it.

MR. LANCET: Mr. Motion, isn't it true you tried to get me to sell you drugs from my foundation? *The* foundation, excuse me.

MR. MOTION: I plead the fifth.

MR. LANCET: Did you not drive me to get those drugs?

MR. MOTION: Plead the fifth.

MR. LANCET: We've been hearing a lot of that today. Wait, were you in on all of this?

MR. MOTION: No. We never would have met if you didn't drop that stuff off.

MR. LANCET: Yeah, but I never would have been there at all if Damian didn't send me to drop those boxes off! Maybe it wasn't the wrong address.

MR. MOTION: Nah, it was the wrong address.

MR. LANCET: Oh. Yeah, I guess that makes sense. So you said that I was hateful and antisemitic against black people, is that correct?

MR. MOTION: You said stuff about women and antisemitic stuff, yeah.

MR. LANCET: Okay, but like, Eli is Jewish, super rich, works in high levels in the media, and he tried to kill me. So it does seem rational to me that he's in a cabal of some kind… Does it not?

MR. MOTION: Dude, no. He might have tried to kill you. I don't know. But this whole thing was your family business. It didn't have to do with being Jewish. Bruh.

MR. LANCET: My bad. It's logical when you receive new information to change your mind. So please let the members of the jury know that I am not antisemitic or racist or anything like that. No go? All right, I guess I have no more questions.

———

MS. BOBBERS: Now calling to the stand Ms. Tomiina Deatherage. Ms. Deatherage, what do you do for a living?

MS. DEATHERAGE: I'm a multi-hyphenate artist. Mostly an actress.

MS. BOBBERS: I see. How do you know Mr. Lancet?

MS. DEATHERAGE: We met during my family's stay at the Hotel Bellehaven.

MS. BOBBERS: And how would you describe your relationship with Mr. Lancet?

MS. DEATHERAGE: It's complicated.

MS. BOBBERS: Are you just friends?

MS. DEATHERAGE: We're close.

MS. BOBBERS: Sorry to press, but given the severity of this case, I'll need you to be more specific. Was there any romantic involvement?

MS. DEATHERAGE: It was a little too early to say.

THE COURT: Mr. Lancet, sit down.

MS. BOBBERS: But you're close?

MS. DEATHERAGE: Yes.

MS. BOBBERS: The reason I ask is that it seems like an odd pairing, don't you agree?

MS. DEATHERAGE: I'm not sure I understand.

MS. BOBBERS: Well, you're beautiful and famous, and he's…

MS. DEATHERAGE: Thank you for saying that, you're sweet. When you're in the entertainment industry, it can be hard to find people who don't want something from you. Lionel hadn't seen any of my movies. He never asked for a picture to show off to all of his friends. It was refreshing.

MS. BOBBERS: So he had friends?

MR. LANCET: Objection, I've got plenty of friends.

THE COURT: Mr. Lancet, your objections need to pertain to fair practice in court. You'll get your time to speak.

MS. BOBBERS: To what degree were you involved in the Fiduciary Royalties Association for United Donors?

MS. DEATHERAGE: I was not involved.

MS. BOBBERS: In any way?

MS. DEATHERAGE: Not in any way.

MS. BOBBERS: Did your father ever mention his stake in the foundation?

MS. DEATHERAGE: No.

MS. BOBBERS: Where is he now?

MS. DEATHERAGE: That is unclear.

MS. BOBBERS: Are you aware that it reported he flew away in a helicopter?

MS. BOBBERS: That sounds like something he would do.

MS. BOBBERS: Did he ever express any dissatisfaction with his business interests?

MS. DEATHERAGE: He kept all of that to himself. Except for the movies, of course.

MS. BOBBERS: Were you aware of any resentment he might have had against the Lancets?

MS. DEATHERAGE: He never mentioned any.

MS. BOBBERS: Did he ever mention a plan to conspire against anyone?

MS. DEATHERAGE: No.

MS. BOBBERS: Did you ever work with your father?

MS. DEATHERAGE: No.

MS. BOBBERS: Is it possible you worked to aid your father's interests in a way that you might not have known pertained to the Fiduciary Royalties Association for United Donors?

MS. DEATHERAGE: No. My criticism of my father and his work has been widely publicized.

MS. BOBBERS: Yes, that's right. I read that you have ideological differences. Is that fair to say?

MS. DEATHERAGE: That's one way of putting it.

MS. BOBBERS: Could you describe those differences?

MS. DEATHERAGE: My father makes trashy blockbusters that depict women horribly. I try to do the opposite.

MS. BOBBERS: That seems like noble work.

MS. DEATHERAGE: I'm pleased with it.

MS. BOBBERS: If you could excuse me for getting perhaps too philosophical, could you describe the central thrust of your message?

MS. DEATHERAGE: My message?

MS. BOBBERS: Yes. For your films. Specifically the more politically engaged films.

MS. DEATHERAGE: It would be to show women in a positive light and give them agency.

MS. BOBBERS: A woman after my own heart.

MS. BOBBERS: In these films, are there villains? Or are they solely about women?

MS. DEATHERAGE: Villains? Antagonists, definitely.

MS. BOBBERS: Could you describe these antagonists?

MS. DEATHERAGE: There are quite a few movies we're talking about here.

MS. BOBBERS: Sure. Details aside, but could you describe them demographically?

MS. DEATHERAGE: I suppose… They are mostly privileged straight white males.

MS. BOBBERS: They are, aren't they? Now Lionel is a straight white male, yes? And privileged?

MS. DEATHERAGE: As far as I know.

MS. BOBBERS: Is it fair to say, that in spite of your ideological differences with your father, the two of you might have found a common enemy in Lionel?

MS. DEATHERAGE: No.

MS. BOBBERS: No?

MS. DEATHERAGE: Yes.

MS. BOBBERS: I'm sorry, I don't understand.

MS. DEATHERAGE: I was saying yes to you asking if I was saying no.

MS. BOBBERS: So there was no collusion with your father against Mr. Lancet?

MS. DEATHERAGE: Correct.

MS. BOBBERS: Now, might you have tried to act against Lionel for your own interests?

MS. DEATHERAGE: Act against him?

MS. BOBBERS: As a matter of activism.

MS. DEATHERAGE: I had no reason to do anything against Lionel.

MS. BOBBERS: But you did say straight white males were the villains in your films.

MS. DEATHERAGE: Antagonists, yes.

MS. BOBBERS: Listen, I'm with you. I would say they are the antagonists not just in your films. I think you and I are similar. But perhaps with a small difference.

MS. DEATHERAGE: Yes?

MS. BOBBERS: Let's say you did try to get at Lionel in some way, in coordination with your father or as a matter of your own activism. This is a good cause. I'm fighting a similar battle against them. But can you spot the difference?

MS. DEATHERAGE: I'm afraid I can't.

MS. BOBBERS: Well, what happens if I win against the Lancets and their foundation?

MS. DEATHERAGE: I'm not sure.

MS. BOBBERS: They would have to take responsibility. All of them. Yes?

MS. DEATHERAGE: I suppose.

MS. BOBBERS: But in the hypothetical scenario of you acting against Lionel on behalf of your father, if you won, what would happen?

MS. DEATHERAGE: I can't answer that.

MS. BOBBERS: Your father profits, no? And he avoids taking responsibility himself.

MR. LANCET: That's actually a pretty good point.

THE COURT: Mr. Lancet, I will not ask you again.

MS. BOBBERS: Was Lionel anything like his grandfather? Any spiritual inclinations?

MS. DEATHERAGE: I believe he was an atheist.

MS. BOBBERS: Was?

MS. DEATHERAGE: He had a change of heart after a psychedelic trip.

MS. BOBBERS: Very interesting.

MS. DEATHERAGE: The same drug created and distributed by his foundation?

MS. DEATHERAGE: I don't know.

MS. BOBBERS: How do you know he took the drug?

MS. DEATHERAGE: He told me. And he said that we are two shards of the godhead, separated into individual bodies, tasked with finding each other and returning to source consciousness so we can be together forever.

MS. BOBBERS: So it's fair to say Mr. Lancet believed you were romantically involved?

MS. DEATHERAGE: Yes. That's actually the word he used. *Involved.*

MS. BOBBERS: I have no further questions.

MR. LANCET: So Ms. Deatherage, did you give me any reason to believe we were involved?

MS. DEATHERAGE: I can't take responsibility for what you believe.

MR. LANCET: Ok, that's logical. But could you tell the lovely people here on the jury what you did the night you came over to my villa?

MS. DEATHERAGE: I gave you a tarot reading.

MR. LANCET: Yeah, but what else?

MS. DEATHERAGE: I made drinks?

MR. LANCET: Okay, yeah, but what else?

MS. DEATHERAGE: I don't remember.

MR. LANCET: Did you lean over the table and kiss me?

MS. DEATHERAGE: Yes.

MR. LANCET: Sounds romantic to me!

MS. BOBBERS: Objection. We have no reason to believe Lionel could pull a woman like Tomiina.

THE COURT: Overruled.

MR. LANCET: She said it herself.

MS. DEATHERAGE: Well, just because we kissed doesn't mean there was any involvement.

MR. LANCET: Fine by me. Just as long as everybody knows. Ms. Deatherage, do remember what Melanie said about you working with your father?

MS. DEATHERAGE: Yeah, it was only like two minutes ago.

MR. LANCET: Yes, so… did you?

MS. DEATHERAGE: Did I what?

MR. LANCET: Work with your father?

MS. DEATHERAGE: In what way?

MR. LANCET: To pin all this on me? Or kill me?

MS. DEATHERAGE: No.

MR. LANCET: Aha! That's right. You're your own person, right?

MS. DEATHERAGE: That's correct.

MR. LANCET: You don't need someone else telling you what to do, right? Especially not a man.

MS. DEATHERAGE: Right.

MR. LANCET: That's right! It would be sexist for Melanie Bobbers to think that you couldn't make your own decisions. So Melanie is sexist against men *and* women.

MS. BOBBERS: Objection. Leading the witness.

THE COURT: Sustained. Mr. Lancet, this is your time to question Ms. Deatherage, not make your own statements.

MS. BOBBERS: Not to mention, it's sexist to think she couldn't do anything wrong.

MR. LANCET: Objection.

THE COURT: Sustained.

MR. LANCET: Is that good?

THE COURT: I agree with your objection, Mr. Lancet. Ms. Bobbers was speaking out of turn. However, it is inappropriate for you to lick your finger and tally points for yourself in the air.

MR. LANCET: Noted. So on the night I was almost murdered, you and I spoke, correct?

MS. DEATHERAGE: Yes.

MR. LANCET: Oh shit. Did you lure me there?

MS. DEATHERAGE: No.

MR. LANCET: Thank god. But we didn't get a chance to finish our conversation, right?

MS. DEATHERAGE: That's right.

MR. LANCET: Where did you go after they threw that bag over my head and dragged me to the theater?

MS. DEATHERAGE: I ran for help.

MR. LANCET: I appreciate that. Could we continue our conversation at some point in the near future?

MS. DEATHERAGE: I think I need more time.

MR. LANCET: That's not a no.

THE COURT: Are you finished, Mr. Lancet?

MR. LANCET: I mean… I guess. Should I keep going?

THE COURT: That's not for me to decide, Mr. Lancet.

MR. LANCET: Okay. I'm finished. And thanks for doing this today.

————

MS. BOBBERS: Now calling to the stand, Lionel Lancet. Mr. Lancet, what is your role in the Fiduciary Royalties Association for United Donors?

MR. LANCET: I never had much to do with The Fiduciary Royalties… my grandpa's foundation.

MS. BOBBERS: Yes, but you did have a role in the foundation, did you not?

MR. LANCET: Yeah, but I didn't even know about it.

MS. BOBBERS: Okay, but what was your role?

MR. LANCET: President. At least, that's what I've been told.

MS. BOBBERS: In your role as president, did you approve the foundation's significant monetary contributions to conservative causes?

MR. LANCET: No. I was not aware of any contributions.

MS. BOBBERS: I'd like to direct the jury's attention to this exhibit. For anyone unfamiliar with this, this is a ledger collecting all of the contributions to right-wing think tanks that advance climate change disinformation campaigns, political ads that sway local elections toward the red, and corporate-sponsored citizens action committees that protest against progressive policies. And it is Mr. Lancet's claim, here today, that he, as president of the foundation, had nothing to do with his foundation's contributions. But tell us, Mr. Lancet, what are your politics?

MR. LANCET: I'm kind of more interested in ideas.

MS. BOBBERS: Sure. But could .you describe the general bent of the ideas you subscribe to?

MR. LANCET: I guess I'm a classical liberal.

MS. BOBBERS: So you're a fan of free speech?

MR. LANCET: Yeah.

MS. BOBBERS: What about free speech do you like?

MR. LANCET: I mean, it's the cornerstone of Western civilization.

MS. BOBBERS: Ah yes, The West. Do you like the West, Mr. Lancet?

MR. LANCET: I think it's important to preserve, yes.

MS. BOBBERS: Preserve or conserve?

MR. LANCET: Either I guess.

MS. BOBBERS: Are you aware that 'The West' is often a dog whistle for white supremacy?

MR. LANCET: What? No. I just like the philosophical tradition. Plato and stuff.

MS. BOBBERS: Could you describe the religious aspects of your foundation?

MR. LANCET: I don't even really know if they had anything to do with the foundation. You're seriously asking the wrong guy.

MS. BOBBERS: Are you saying they were separate?

MR. LANCET: I don't know if they were or not is what I'm saying. Like, I was never clear on what the foundation was for. The religious part seemed pretty out there.

MS. BOBBERS: But you are aware that there were sacrificial rituals performed by members of the foundation, are you not?

MR. LANCET: Yeah. It just seems surprising. They were a bunch of businessmen.

MS. BOBBERS: Do you mean white men?

MR. LANCET: No. I mean, I guess they were white, but I just mean I wouldn't have guessed they were into all of that stuff.

MS. BOBBERS: What stuff?

MR. LANCET: Like, trippy drugs and stuff.

MS. BOBBERS: And ritual sacrifice?

MR. LANCET: Yeah. That caught me way off guard. One minute I'm talking to Tomiina in the lobby of the hotel and the next I'm about to get murdered.

MS. BOBBERS: Were you the one who organized the attempt on my life?

MR. LANCET: No. They tried to get me too.

MS. BOBBERS: So how do you justify the sacrifice's separation from the foundation's conservative politics?

MR. LANCET: I don't think I understand.

MS. BOBBERS: I would argue their conservative agenda and their sacrificial rituals are linked. Do you disagree?

MR. LANCET: I don't know. I mean, their ideas stand on their own, right? Like, my foun —the foundation didn't invent these ideas, whether they tried to spread them or not, which I knew nothing about, by the way. And like I said, I'm not a conservative, but I don't see how their sacrificial rituals had anything to do with being conservative.

MS. BOBBERS: In due time, Lionel. Could you explain what the goal was of the ceremony you did with your grandfather's maid and your friend Tony Motion?

MR. LANCET: How do you know about that?

MS. BOBBERS: It's my time to question you, Mr. Lancet. What was the purpose of the ceremony?

MR. LANCET: I guess it was to go beyond the material world.

MS. BOBBERS: Transcendence?

MR. LANCET: Yeah. That's fair.

MS. BOBBERS: If I understand, this transcendence required drugs. Is that correct?

MR. LANCET: Yeah.

MS. BOBBERS: Could you describe the transcendent state for the jury?

MR. LANCET: It showed me that I, as a person, was not what I thought I was.

MS. BOBBERS: What did you think you were before?

MR. LANCET: Just my body, I guess.

MS. BOBBERS: And now?

MR. LANCET: It's like I'm a spiritual being.

MS. BOBBERS: A god?

MR. LANCET: I mean it sounds crazy, but yeah. It might be a metaphor. I don't know. It's not exactly logical, but I feel like it's not a scientific claim. It's a new way I see myself. Like a divine being. But so are you, and so is everyone. Not just me.

MS. BOBBERS: That's very touching. But—

MR. LANCET: Like, it used to seem like there was an active conspiracy against me, from all other people, like everyone was against me, and everything too, like, even the world around me.

MS. BOBBERS: Now, I'd like to—

MR. LANCET: You know, it's funny. I had no confidence, and I really thought that I was this innocent victim and that I couldn't be arrogant or entitled. Those things are for the people who get what they want. I'm not a coward, I'm just a nice guy in a world that won't ever recognize it. Things like that. But I was wrong. I thought other people fighting for what they wanted and standing up for themselves was them being mean and arrogant and entitled. But I was the one who was that way. I thought I was entitled to go through life without conflict, without ever having to work hard or try.

MS. BOBBERS: Okay.

MR. LANCET: So here I sit, confronting my fate.

MS. BOBBERS: How inspiring. Did you learn all of that on the drug?

MR. LANCET: Yes. And I practiced it a little on the way here.

MS. BOBBERS: I'd like to direct the jury's attention to this exhibit that shows what Lionel's transcendent experience actually was.

Melanie projected a video taken from her lapel camera as she crouched in the bushes on the perimeter of Art's backyard. The video showed Lionel lying on the ground, flailing about, squealing like an animal. Several times, he got on his feet to chase something that wasn't there, before tripping and falling to the ground in a heap. Then the puking started. He heaved loudly, and each expulsion of vomit seemed to cause him great pain. He was crying openly and puking between sobs. Constance tried to help him until he puked all over her face. She stood and left him to his delirium.

The members of the jury squinted their eyes and cocked their heads to fully take in what they were watching. Some people turned away at the sight of his puking. An elderly man in suspenders grinned openly, shook his head, and crossed his arms.

Melanie paused the video.

MS. BOBBERS: This goes on for a while, but I think you get the idea. So Mr. Lancet, it seems you participated in your foundation's ceremony. And yet you maintain you were uninvolved with the foundation?

MR. LANCET: That's correct.

MS. BOBBERS: Now, when I deposed you, you told me you were an atheist. Is that correct?

MR. LANCET: Yes.

MS. BOBBERS: Could you explain your former atheism to me?

MR. LANCET: After hearing the evidence, or lack of evidence, for the existence of God, I didn't believe. I used to watch Richard Dawkins and Christopher Hitchens and Sam Harris videos on YouTube, and they convinced me.

MS. BOBBERS: So you like people who cut down believers without mercy?

MR. LANCET: I'll admit, I found that very entertaining. I still do. But I think that they're important thinkers too. Religious institutions have done some terrible things, and it's necessary to have people who are willing to call that out. Like I said, I'm a classical liberal. I don't like big institutions committing evil.

MS. BOBBERS: Are you aware Christopher Hitchens supported the Iraq War?

MR. LANCET: Do you think I had something to do with the Iraq War?

MS. BOBBERS: That exceeds the purview of this trial. Also, Sam Harris has spoken in support of the State of Israel.

MR. LANCET: Well, it's a bit more complex than that.

MS. BOBBERS: It seems that your new spirituality is a pretty big departure from your previous worldview, is it not?

MR. LANCET: I mean yeah. But I don't think anything I've said is inconsistent with science.

MS. BOBBERS: So you're saying if we disagree with you today, we're disagreeing with science?

MR. LANCET: Yes. Uh, it depends. Disagree about what? Are you saying if we disagree with you, we disagree with the plight of the oppressed?

MS. BOBBERS: That's extremely offensive.

MR. LANCET: Objection?

THE COURT: Sustained. Please don't opine about the defendant's responses, Ms. Bobbers.

MS. BOBBERS: Yes, your honor. Now, this document is the notarized transfer of assets to the Cayman Islands I showed earlier. Is that your signature at the bottom?

MR. LANCET: Yeah, it looks like it.

MS. BOBBERS: Do you remember signing it and getting it notarized?

MR. LANCET: Yeah, but I didn't know what it was. I thought it was for the hotel.

MS. BOBBERS: Yes, the hotel you and your grandfather have a financial stake in. Correct?

MR. LANCET: I guess. I actually didn't know I had a financial stake in it. Do I?

MS. BOBBERS: So you maintain you were uninvolved in the foundation even though you went to a notary public to finalize a transfer of assets to the Cayman Islands?

MR. LANCET: I didn't know what it was. Damian had me do it.

MS. BOBBERS: And earlier it appears that Mr. Motion discussed a delivery of legal documents to his address. Is that correct?

MR. LANCET: Yeah.

MS. BOBBERS: Which you took there by mistake, according to him. Are you aware of who lives directly next door to Tony Motion?

MR. LANCET: No clue. But I didn't know what was in those boxes. Damian had me deliver them.

MS. BOBBERS: Are you aware that the house next to Tony Motion belongs to Eli Deatherage?

MR. LANCET: Oh Wow. That makes a lot of sense. No. I did not.

MS. BOBBERS: After realizing your mistake, did you ever complete the delivery?"

MR. LANCET: No.

MS. BOBBERS: So what happened to those documents?

MR. LANCET: I burned them.

MS. BOBBERS: You destroyed them?

MR. LANCET: I read a few of them first, but yeah. I threw them in my fireplace.

MS. BOBBERS: Why did you do that?

MR. LANCET: I don't know. It just seemed kinda weird that Damian was sending documents around about me, so I thought I'd get rid of them.

MS. BOBBERS: Did you burn them because you thought they might contain incriminating evidence against you?

MR. LANCET: No. It was really a spur-of-the-moment decision.

MS. BOBBERS: Did you think Mr. Motion might act against you?

MR. LANCET: I honestly don't think he had anything to do with it.

MS. BOBBERS: That may be the case, but it seems that you and Mr. Motion took a trip near Joshua Tree. Do you recall doing this?

MR. LANCET: Yeah.

MS. BOBBERS: Could you describe the place you visited?

MR. LANCET: Yeah, it was weird. It was like this place with all these domes and these dudes with guns and walkie-talkies were everywhere.

MS. BOBBERS: Would you describe this as a militia encampment?

MR. LANCET: I mean, I guess. I didn't really know what it was.

MS. BOBBERS: Did you fund this militia?

MR. LANCET: I didn't even know about it until we went. And I definitely didn't expect to see my dad there.

MS. BOBBERS: Your father was at the militia encampment?

MR. LANCET: Yeah, he was hiding out there. Honestly, you should question him. He would know way more about all this than I do.

MS. BOBBERS: Why did you go to this militia encampment?

MR. LANCET: We wanted to get the Adhik—the drugs we took.

MS. BOBBERS: Did you buy them from them?

MR. LANCET: Well, technically they were already mine. I didn't know that, but when we got there, it was the wrong address. It was all Tony's idea.

MS. BOBBERS: And where did you find the drugs after discovering they weren't at your militia encampment?

MR. LANCET: It wasn't mine. But we went to my grandpa's house. We found them there.

MS. BOBBERS: Your grandfather, the one who started the foundation?

MR. LANCET: Yes.

MS. BOBBERS: I have no further questions.

———

THE COURT: Ms. Bobbers, you may now make your closing statement.

MS. BOBBERS: What we have here is a decision to make. We must decide if Lionel Lancet is guilty. Guilty of avoiding his debt to society through a tax dodge masquerading as a charitable foundation. Guilty of pedaling conservative ideas by funding think tanks that convince average Americans that they'll be affected by attempts to tax the richest of the rich. Guilty of funding a right-wing militia, and most importantly, guilty of running a foundation that murders its victims in ritual sacrifices.

If the evidence shows that he is in fact not guilty, then by all means, he should be set free to live his life. But I'm afraid the evidence shows otherwise. We have the defendant admitting that he notarized a transfer of assets to an account in the Cayman Islands. The owner of that account is anybody's guess, but you heard him admit he did as much. The defendant also appears to have destroyed documents relating to his foundation. How do we know? Again, the defendant told us he did. No speculation involved. Furthermore, he told us that he visited a right-wing militia that his foundation bankrolled. We heard it from the man himself. And lastly, he told everyone here today that he picked up drugs from his grandfather's house and participated in the ceremony that is central to his foundation.

I believe it is clear based on Mr. Lancet's behavior here in court that the seeming spiritual shift he claims he had is nothing more than an exaggerated report of a hallucinogenic drug experience, an attempt to distance himself from his privilege, and an obvious attempt to strike at the sympathy of the jury. What might seem like a psychedelic, New Age rebel who has broken away from the legacy of his ancestors is nothing more than conservatism repackaged and shape-shifted for modern times. Lionel's beliefs are like a religion that his favorite atheists are against: it's backed by a powerful institution, it pedals damaging ideas, and it has a trail of blood in its wake. Do not be fooled. Beneath the surface is the same old

Boomer mentality that has ruined the world. We have no reason to believe that Lionel is any different from his grandfather or the track record that he has established: helming a foundation that marries the worst of conservatism and ritual sacrifice by cheating on taxes, spreads right-wing ideas through militias and terrorism, and sacrifices the lives of others, all for personal gain. Lionel pleads ignorance to these actions, but he has done nothing to avoid recapitulating them. He believes in them only when they come after him. I am asking the jury to hold the defendant guilty and the judge to punish him to the fullest extent of the law.

THE COURT: Mr. Lancet, you may now make your closing statement.

MR. LANCET: I've got to hand it to Melanie. There's no doubt that when it comes to the law, she knows a lot more than me about this stuff. If I were on the jury, I'd probably agree with her. So I can't really expect anyone to believe me. In fact for a second, how about we take that off the table? I don't care if you believe me or not.

When I drank that drug at my grandfather's house, as you all saw… I know it looked silly, but what I saw was that there's a whole lot more going on here than what we think. It opened my eyes to something, and I think I can open your eyes to it too. If you're willing. I may be privileged. That's probably true. I may be a white man. But I consider it this white man's burden to lift you up with what I've seen. And with what I've learned I am. It seems that I am a higher being. I am a god of some sort. But so is everyone, many of you probably just haven't seen it yet. It's a force you can access, a whole dimension we've been neglecting. The human race is way more than what we've been told we are. We're a master race actually, and together we can build a great society. It sounds crazy, I know.

Because what's more likely, that we are born to work to eat to sleep and die, or that we are born to access the light inside of ourselves? And I know you say it's all in my head. But where else would it be? I'll tell you. In the world around you! That is the goal of our light, to use it to turn what's in our heads into reality. The world around us seems dead, but lurking behind everything there is a soul and a spirit.

So am I the president of a murderous foundation? Yes. Did I send that transfer of assets to the Cayman Islands and burn the documents and all that stuff? Yes. But I ask the jury to see their own internal light in this moment. Because while I don't grasp all of the facts, I do have my values and my principles. And I can see that the answer here is kindness.

MS. BOBBERS: You just admitted guilt?

THE COURT: People of the jury, do you all need time to deliberate?

JUROR: No, I think we're all in agreement.

JUROR: Guilty.

JUROR: Oh yeah, 100% guilty.

MR. LANCET: Shit.

Part IV
The Kingdom of Heaven and Earth

Chapter 22

In Los Angeles, the sun shines daily, and the smog has apparently thinned due to environmental regulations and emissions control, but from high up, its yellow-brown layer delineates itself against the sky. Innumerable particulates swarm with every inhale but catch and spread the light nicely. With no snow, Christmas sneaks up every year, and a gathering "last week" is revealed to have taken place more than six months ago. The sunny paradise pinches off the timeline on which the rest of the world proceeds and either stops or barrels headlong in its own direction.

The palms and vibrant fruits still manage to decay and drupe down, from festive brilliance to tacky faded thatch, and people approaching in the distance look youthful until they get closer and it emerges they are middle-aged, as though decades passed as they closed the short distance, still dressed in the countercultural fashions of their bygone eras. Each is a small portal to the past.

Plaster adobe and boxy modern houses share residential blocks, not a transition or phasing out the old for the new, but a coexistence of two eras. Shaggy hair and mutton chops bob up and down next to post-millennium coiffures as their owners stride down the sidewalk. Floral shirts, circular John Lennon glasses, and VW vans circulate, hardly a throwback as their heyday has only just begun.

It's the City of Angels, but the city's ghosts dominate, spirits of the powerful few and all those in their wake. They don't emerge from the past. They never left. Either embedded in the topography of the land or conjured by the people on it, past, present, and future are concurrent, blurred, inseparable.

Such a metaphysical state makes progress elusive for a society. The past is nothing that can be escaped and the future, already decided. As for the present, any temporal connotation gives way to that of location, bound by a city that moves only during an earthquake, while the backdrop manifests as eternity.

Every sign that the men in charge are about to get their comeuppance is undermined by that which is consistent in the developed landscape. Just what is consistent is hard to say, an unacknowledged absence, a lack in the heart of every striving bastard. All passing thrills and hopes subside and remind the city at large that the same old captain is steering the ship until the tide rises and fills the Los Angeles basin.

With the destruction of traditional gods and the outing of deviants in religious institutions, not to mention atheism's inability to satisfy humanity's need to drink alcohol, light things on fire, and insist that the occasion transcended the material plane, the Fiduciary Royalties Association for United Donors sought to integrate the empirical rigor of the sciences with the more nebulous spiritual needs of lived experience, and in effect, do away with the criticism that noted God's glaring absence.

In a document that Lionel burned on his villa's porch, exorcising the spirit of the words from their textual symbols, Art Lancet shared the intentions of his foundation:

It started as a few of us running around in the woods, chasing the sensation where the surrounding world seemed to take on an eerie sense of significance, as though something elusive and playful rose off of every object like smoke. Its formless effusion provided an attractive enclosure, a coy feminine absence to disappear into and hide away from the sense of presence that always left us exposed. But how fickle the goddess proved to be, and for all the beauty of her shifting, unbounded by matter, it was this precisely that made her untrustworthy, hinting that complete union with her would mean death.

In order to achieve this transcendent moment while managing such a grave risk and eternal liability, it was necessary to get organized. Codified. Incorporating as a foundation made the whole process more reliable. But we are not a think-tank or symposium. Nor are we academics. Proof and persuasion are none of our business. And for all of our supra-material inclinations, we don't proselytize.

It's not wholly unscientific. If anything, it's our aim to make transcendence replicable. So we took it upon ourselves, through extensive experimentation, to come up with a system to conjure this transcendence with sacrament. We could not afford empty ritual. We wanted our sacraments to work. We were interested in actual transcendence, the bottom line, the royalties.

I came to believe that every object is imbued with a power that exceeds this material plane and contains the spirit of what many consider a god (a goddess in this case). This narrative is actually less theistic than it might seem. It is more of an application of polytheism to an epistemology of objects, a new animism for our time. I grew sick of skeptics dismissing literal objects as dead, inanimate things and criticizing the phenomenology of objects as constructions or projections of the mind (as if that made them less real).

With this radical deification of all objects, let's allow ourselves to be more clever than to ponder the numinous properties of a chair or a table; these dull examples inevitability make their way into every philosophical discussion. Mightn't the canon of things called real be all the more clear and compelling if it were to advance past perceptual navel-gazing about the reality of furniture and appliances and instead induct into its ranks the contents of our interiors, where we are all the most similar? Naming all the colorful shades of emotion, identity, ego, and dream might accelerate everything. It's of greater interest to us all to apprehend these less tangible objects that more closely resemble philosophical objects of consideration— emotions, love, justice, truth, the soul. In moments of doubt, I know these only as absence, but the ubiquity of their presence is what obscures their imposition into everything.

At my greatest moments of weakness, I wish to turn my back on all of the goddess's mysteries and return to the certainty of science, measuring phenomena and acknowledging the limits of observation and perception as a mere technical formality. There is something comforting and empowering about feeling the weight of a tangible object. It lets us sink our teeth into something substantial, but for all my best attempts to know the goddess as real, I was always reduced to a suckling baby, gumming at an incorporeal essence.

And I am forced to acknowledge that carving up the mother goddess and packaging her into rites, doctrines, and mantras objectifies her power which can only exist as a field of undifferentiated energy. I don't deny the limitations of knowing her through my lens. We're able to see only one part of her at a time, a mere surface, like a higher dimensional object passing through the lower dimensions. We're never granted more than a glimpse. She endlessly escapes us.

Belief is something I never considered too closely, as a term anyway, because all of my mystical experiences evaded my interpretations. Interpretation is usually what people are asking about when they question beliefs. Mention the goddess to someone, and they'll immediately start arguing with the assumption that she can be verified with the senses. My inclusion of the mother goddess as a numinous object in the narrative I developed is an interpretation admittedly, but it should not be confused with what she actually is. I'm merely using words to trace the shape of something invisible and omnipresent, allowing us to lean over the edge of the outline and peer into a realm where words no longer apply. Perhaps to know her completely would require jumping off, bidding the safety and comfort of the material world goodbye and parting ways with the imperfect significance of words that let us dangle out over the void.

Take comfort that when I am dead and gone, I will know her at last. In the meantime, I'll make peace with the empty words. They provide an account of the holiness of objects, however imperfect. Perhaps they're an artifice with a hollow interior, but they're useful. They're worth preserving and passing down. No one, and certainly no centralized structure, should be trusted to divvy up what they try to take from this legacy. It's my life's work and my contribution to the world, and I'll be damned before it's sullied or stolen. My entitled descendants will never know the work I had to do to bring it into existence, and I often wonder if Constance aims to have it for herself. Every woman hides her secrets. I've come to suspect they're all trying to destroy me.

The edges of the coffee table in Constance's living room expanded in Lionel's vision. It was just a small vestige of his trip over the horizon, the details of which got blurrier with each passing day. For as transformative as it seemed, Lionel could go for several hours at a time without remembering that it showed him dimensions beyond material surfaces including that which transcended his body, the part of him that was divine. He would bring it all back to his mind and focus on it as the key to all of his decisions going forward.

But after the excitement of the trial died down, almost nothing in his life required whatever skillset he thought he gleaned from ingesting the brew. He began to doubt that it showed him anything in particular, reasoning that he simply concocted a story about a hallucinatory drug experience brought on from scrambling his brain chemistry. Words couldn't describe whatever it was, and science could only account for which lobes and synapses the brew egged on. But still, he felt it all.

He became quite talkative, specifically about his experiences under the influence of the brew; if his first experience taught him that there was a supra-material dimension to the universe, future ceremonies might address his newfound problem of talking over his interlocutors and verbally bludgeoning them with empty philosophical musings and confusing attempts at voicing the ineffable.

Lionel lay back on the couch, resigning himself to the realization that the trip to the other side of surfaces, real or imagined, was unfortunately unreliable. He stretched his legs out to rest on the coffee table, drawing his joggers past a bracelet with a blinking battery pack strapped beneath his shin. But his legs fell short of the coffee table's edge, which shifted still in his vision.

He had never been graceful, but it pained him to know his foot-eye coordination was insufficient, even preventing him from relaxing properly. He eyed the whole room with distrust. Each object was a pair with something hovering above it: one hard and certain and the other shifting and mysterious. Even trying to say just what was hovering stripped it of its essence. And for practical purposes, Lionel often had to focus just on the objects. But when he was willing to relax, the hovering somethings emerged, only to dart away the moment he tried to look at them, like a floater on his eyeball.

The hard surfaces of objects used to promise some sort of fixity, stable ground to stand on, or slump on in his case. But they now seemed as distant and false as his fading memories of transcendence on the psychedelic brew. Focusing on the material world, this narrow spectrum of phenomena, left the rest of him barren, opening space for indoctrination into a conservative legacy that approached him from inside the family and from the algorithm pegging his demographic as the target audience for a network of ideas that tried to offer a bird's eye view of the "facts" whether or not people became mere data points, harvested and sold to advertisers and business interests in an attempt to compete with China. Lionel's body could already be dismissed as an aggregate of percentiles, and a digital version of him existed somewhere in cyberspace, an immaterial soul consisting of his browsing habits and search history, the extent of his being before the brew upgraded his interior with something the data couldn't touch.

He checked his phone. The message he sent Tomiina was left on "delivered." Her spiritual woo and emotional whims erected a wall that Lionel could not peek behind, but for all the mystery of whatever hid on the other side, he decided that she had not conspired to kill him, a belief that was a matter of faith. He didn't see her take the snake-handled dagger from his grandfather's house, and even if he had, he would not have interpreted the foundation trying to stab him with it as proof of her guilt. Someone might have taken it from her possession.

Lionel felt Tomiina's absence and held out hope that the version of himself she provided with her attention would return. Perhaps it was only an enclosure to spill his discombobulated sense of self into, but he liked the way it fit, comforting and containing him. In spite of his best efforts to suppress the thought, it crossed his mind that she needed an enclosure as well, a role to orchestrate a taxonomy of feelings and beliefs for her. But she didn't need him for that. She had her tarot cards and the characters she played in her films.

Lionel saw an ad for her next film, *Trite Savior*, a satire in which Tomiina plays a white progressive actress who turns the plight of the oppressed into self-serving financial opportunities, one film at a time. He wasn't entrenched in the world of progressivism enough to know whether she was trying to show that she was aware of her own actions in this regard or if she was calling out white saviors with whom she did not identify. In either case, she marked herself with a sign in hopes that the spirit of militant progressivism would pass over her and target someone else. *Trite Savior* already generated a lot of buzz on Twitter, and it would surely turn a profit.

Eli Deatherage funded the production in an attempt to make peace with his daughter, but he regretfully informed her that he could not risk traveling to the United States for the premiere. He moved to the Cayman Islands, leaving Susan to take care of their home in Holmby Hills. This bought him the sign of Passover, and Damian, Lee Furnival, and the Lunada Bay Boys would catch whatever punishment was meant for him. Their trials were set for a year from now.

Art evaded justice by having the good sense to die before everything got ugly, and his spiritual veneer and kurta shirts kept him under the radar before that, buying him time to get his affairs in order and organize a union between his roles as a financial guru and a spiritual kingpin. He poured himself into both equally, and perhaps refusing to choose one over the other split him in half. The mark of Passover fixed itself to him until he attempted to alternately deconstruct it and then reify it, trying desperately to prove its symbolic significance was as real as a hydrogen atom.

This was what amounted to a plot to kill Lionel, his only grandson, the would-be heir to the throne if only Lionel showed a stronger interest in capitalizing on the semiotic mystique of the divine. His grandfather did not hate him, in spite of his sincere disappointment in Lionel's childish inability to carry on the family legacy. But it was Art's insistence that he could know the mysteries of the universe in clear terms and put them up for sale that cohered into an agent of death. Each doctrine and mantra became an attempt to commodify numinous experience, which removed all divinity and made space for a more nefarious energy to settle in its spiritual packaging.

Reducing the great beyond to words turns its mysterious nature into a set of facts believers are desperate to protect and conserve. But ironically, grasping a sense of objectivity so tightly is what poisons the inheritance they will to their descendants. It turns the subjective experience of the divine into a set of laws to be enforced, a list of recited principles to justify ownership of the land and the actions required to colonize it.

Certainly, progressive factions made headway interfering with this inheritance, but Melanie's *Little Miss ProseCute* and Tomiina's indulgent performances committed their work to a screen and fixed progress into an aspect ratio and the fluid bliss of their action into a doctrine. But it wasn't real progressives or Melanie Bobbers or Tomiina who cast Lionel as a scapegoat, a sacrificial lamb to die for the sins of his ancestors. It was his ancestors themselves and the story they espoused to legitimize their hoarding and hiding their loot in a corrupt inheritance for future generations.

As the narratives become dogma, their offerings spoil. The communitarian effort turns into individualism with the desire to be the star of history. The stability of conserving the status quo becomes the callous indifference to those who fall through the cracks. So if dogmatic progressivism is egoic indulgence and conservatism a death cult dressed up in khakis and Polos, would it behoove undecided agnostics to meditate on a middle way? Should they negotiate a merger to achieve enlightened centrism? Perhaps their false equivalence exists as a binary only conceptually, features of perception rather than objective measures of truth. Still, their congregations fade into the irrelevance of the natural landscape as a new dogma, in the form of concentrations of data, elevate overlords who will reign over smart cities and provide our basic necessities through subscription: a corporate monarchy presiding over the commune.

For Lionel, it was no longer feasible to rest on a notion of the objective truth. That melted before his eyes after a drink of Adhikashara. But settling on which fiction best suited him still posed a problem. The role as an intellectual he fashioned to himself no longer fit, and the role of a desirable, capable man Tomiina cast him in was missing in action, unless she texted him back. In light of his new deference to the spiritual plane, almost getting murdered in a ritual sacrifice turned him off religion for the foreseeable future. With these fictions exhausted, would he have to invent one of his own? The prospect made his head hurt. He flipped on the TV instead.

A commercial was on for an over-the-counter pain reliever. When it ended, an episodic drama came on, a new guilty pleasure of his. As his strict scientism faded away, he acknowledged that stories, however contrived, allowed him to confront something that he always ignored before since it wasn't a material object: the fear of trying and failing. Maybe Lionel would have a journey of his own someday.

A hand came down on his shoulder, and Lionel flinched. The hand was Constance's. She entered with a cloth and spray bottle of surface cleaner and pointed at an accumulation of crumbs on the coffee table from a bag of veggie chips in front of him.

"I've got it," said Lionel, taking the cleaning supplies from her. He watched the TV while slowly wiping the surface of the table.

Tony popped his head in and said, "Can you clear the table, Lionel?" Lionel rolled his eyes. "I'm not gonna ask you again, young man."

Lionel rose but kept his eyes on the TV, stopping in place to scratch beneath his ankle bracelet. In the kitchen, he scraped the food scraps from plates into the trash and loaded them into the dishwasher.

The master bedroom door was open, and as Lionel wiped down the table, he saw Constance looking in the mirror and brushing her hair. She adjusted the angle of her head for a different view and put her hair behind her ears. When she was satisfied, she removed a set of false teeth from her mouth and set them in their case.

Lionel froze and stared, unable to go on cleaning surfaces. Something rose inside of him too quickly for him to force it back down, and it came out as tears as Constance turned the lights off to go to bed.

Made in the USA
Las Vegas, NV
01 September 2021